THE LAST
WISH LIST

THE LAST WISH LIST

by

Jacqueline Silvester

SIMON & SCHUSTER

London New York Amsterdam/Antwerp Sydney/Melbourne Toronto New Delhi

First published in Great Britain in 2025 by Simon & Schuster UK Ltd

Text copyright © 2025 Jacqueline Silvester

1 3 5 7 9 10 8 6 4 2

Simon & Schuster UK Ltd
1st Floor
222 Gray's Inn Road
London WC1X 8HB

www.simonandschuster.co.uk
www.simonandschuster.com.au
www.simonandschuster.co.in

Simon & Schuster Australia, Sydney
Simon & Schuster India, New Delhi

The authorised representative in the EEA is Simon & Schuster Netherlands BV,
Herculesplein 96, 3584 AA Utrecht, Netherlands. info@simonandschuster.nl

A CIP catalogue record for this book
is available from the British Library

PB ISBN 978-1-3985-3608-1
eBook ISBN 978-1-3985-3637-1
eAudio ISBN 978-1-3985-3636-4

This book is a work of fiction. Names, characters, places and incidents are either
a product of the author's imagination or are used fictitiously. Any resemblance
to actual people living or dead, events or locales is entirely coincidental.

Typeset in Times New Roman by M Rules
Printed and Bound in the UK using 100% Renewable
Electricity at CPI Group (UK) Ltd

MIX
Paper | Supporting
responsible forestry
FSC
www.fsc.org   FSC® C013604

To Viera, my faith
And to Ezra, my hope

'Grief is an unfinished love story'

AUTHOR UNKNOWN

The Last Wish List

1. ~~Ask someone hot out at school~~
2. ~~Scream into the void~~
3. Do something nostalgic
4. Do something that scares you
5. Have a Gosling kiss
6. Eat sweets for dinner
7. Go skinny-dipping
8. Get PJs signed by godlike pop star
9. Play bingo with old ladies
10. Dye your hair a wild colour
11. Go stargazing
12. Stand up for yourself
13. Perform at an open mic night
14. Go viral on social media for doing something cool
15. Toast an achievement with expensive champagne
16. Visit my parents?

CHAPTER 1

My best friend was

Dead girls don't have birthdays.

I glance down at the soggy red velvet cupcake cradled in my hand as if it were a riddle. Why did I buy this? What was I going to do – put a candle in it? Eat it? I look over to the bus stop as if someone could tell me. I was sixteen when I buried my best friend. Now I'm seventeen, and today Lizzy is too. Except she isn't, not really. My thumb pushes into the buttercream.

Red velvet was her favourite.

I should say a few words.

My best friend Lizzy was brave and fierce.

Was.

My best friend Lizzy *is* brave and fierce; she *is* a great dancer, and she *is* never on time.

I want to say *is* so badly, but I can't. My tongue doesn't turn that way any more, but I can't say *was* either, because the truth hurts my tongue even more than the lie.

There is so much in that one word; so much meaning, the difference between someone being, and someone who will never really 'be' again. Someone who will never order cod on vinegar-stained chips from the derelict shop on the high street. Or laugh with me at Mrs Patterson's lipstick teeth. Or hum the words to every Shawn Next song that there is.

Lizzy will never *be*.

My knock-off sneakers are soaked as I wait for the 456 bus. There's not enough room under the bus stop awning for me; it's full of kids and old people. I would rather stand a few feet away, alone, exposed to the rain anyway. It helps me feel sorry for myself. As if I were in a really crappy music video.

I throw the cupcake in the bin and one of the moon-faced toddlers looks at me like I've committed a violent crime.

I'm supposed to visit my uncle and grandma for

dumplings, like I do every Friday afternoon. Fridays go on but Lizzy doesn't. The 456 goes on but Lizzy doesn't. The whole damn world goes on but Lizzy doesn't.

I pull out Lizzy's death list from the pocket of my ratty raincoat. The list is a crumpled up useless thing at this point, and the fat drops of rain ricocheting off my forehead make it worse. I stare at the list – the things Lizzy decided I should do after she died. To get over her or something. I've only marked three so far.

1. ~~Ask someone hot out at school~~
2. ~~Go stargazing~~
3. ~~Scream into the void~~

I didn't even do those things properly. I watched the barely there stars from a supermarket car park, and screamed into that same car park until the staff asked me to leave. And I asked Joey, the star rugby player at St Jude's (who I've had a crush on since fourth form) out with so much resentment that he cowered, actually cowered, and then said a very polite *No, but thank you for thinking of me, Nadia.* As if I had asked him to speak at the opening of the local community centre and he was busy that night. It was the most condolence-like rejection anyone has ever gotten. In the history of the universe.

But what did I expect? The whole school sees me as the girl whose best friend died. That's my brand now.

The bus brings me to the west side of the town and I can feel the smell of my Babushka's meat-and-onion dumplings from the bus stop. It's like a beacon – nothing else smells quite like fresh pelmeni. My grandmother lives at my uncle's house, on the first floor of a block of flats the colour of charcoal. I weave between the Disney scooters and haphazardly parked bikes and knock on the door.

I'm ushered in and quickly put to work.

I help my grandmother with the laying out of the horseradish, sliced kohlrabi, chicken cutlets, diced beetroot, and something we like to call Korean salad – a salad made of grated carrots that I'm pretty sure has absolutely nothing to do with Korea.

My uncle just sits there, polishing an old clock. He tells me he bought it at a car boot sale for a tenner and that it will go for ten times that on 'the eBay'. He thinks it's from the turn of the century. I don't care about the clock.

It annoys me that he never helps with cooking or setting the table. Like he's some kind of king.

Everything has annoyed me for exactly eight months and fourteen days now. But who's counting?

I don't mind helping though. I almost feel better when my hands are moving, when I'm doing something. In my big family there is never a shortage of things to do. When we are like this, simmering, and bustling and serving, I almost feel better. *Almost.*

It's when the doing stops and the talking starts that things start crashing in.

My mama and little brothers arrive twenty minutes later. Mother shoves her heavy coat at me, looking tired, and kisses me on the cheek a little harder than I'd like. I tussle Nikita's curly chestnut hair – he's seven, and he still likes affection. Stepa is a lanky teen now, and he's got a minefield of cystic acne to prove it. He's two years younger than me at fifteen, with eyes the same blue as mine and Nikita's but darker. He's not into physical affection any more. He spares me a smile though.

My dad arrives next, tired from his last plumbing shift. We spread out around the big table. My mum and dad, grandma, uncle, and my two brothers. We fan out, like a palm with stretched-out fingers, with lifelines spreading out and connecting three generations across a table.

My other aunt, Larissa, practically falls through the door, late as always.

'Let me guess, bus was broken, car ran out of fuel, trains weren't running?' my grandmother says. Her head bobs with teasing disapproval.

'Nope, I just didn't really feel like coming. Which usually slows me down,' my glamorous aunt retorts as she grins at me. She unwinds her expensive- looking scarf and hangs it up. My mum glowers at her, but her younger sister just sticks her tongue out and sits down at the table. Throwing her freshly blown-out brown locks over her shoulder. Unbothered.

Larissa is my idol. She used to model, and she wears thigh-high boots under her fox furs. She likes to dabble in tarot and crystals, which, to my mama, means she might as well be walking around with bags of beheaded dolls and speaking in tongues. Larissa divorced her husband after he laid a hand on her; she didn't wait to 'fix it' like everyone instructed her to. To everyone, especially her sister, Larissa is the black sheep in this family. To me she's the free stallion. Galloping in and out of our boring lives.

Too glamorous to be guilted.

'Everybody is here,' says Grandma. 'Let's start.'

Her eyes dart to the mantel when she says *everybody*.

The only person missing is my uncle Tomya; he passed away before I was born. But an icon and candle keep vigil next to his portrait in the living room. I don't know much about him, and Grandma rarely brings him up. But sometimes I catch her looking that way.

'How is Pasha's football practice going?' my papa asks as his honey eyes settle on my uncle, whose son is a supposed future football star.

'Good, he will be scouted soon no doubt,' my uncle declares proudly, as if it's his achievement that the son who has never lived with him is good at sports.

'We will be watching him on the telly soon, playing for Chelsea!' my mum declares.

'I don't care what club Pasha picks as long as I get free tickets,' says my eldest brother through a mouthful of chicken cutlet.

'If I were a footballer I'd play for Everton!' declares my youngest brother.

My uncle gives him a pitying look. 'You're not a footballer though, are you?'

Nikita's face deflates. And I suddenly wish it were

socially acceptable to punch members of your family in the face.

But I don't. I don't really do or say anything at these dinners any more. I just kind of move things around my bowl. Drowning my dumplings in their own sour-cream-tinged broth.

Part of me knows it's unreasonable to expect them to remember that it's Lizzy's birthday today. In Eastern European cultures people are obsessed with death; my mother still mentions how old her grandfather would have turned each year. 'Today he would have been 102!' she would say mournfully once a year. But something tells me they won't remember Lizzy's birthday. Because it's my pain, it's not theirs.

But I wish they did.

We don't talk about Lizzy at all.

We talk about the elections in Eastern Europe, even though it doesn't affect us directly. We talk about how cold it has been (even though we have Siberian roots). My family complains about a neighbour's litter, in the single most hypocritical conversation ever, because they refuse to recycle properly despite my begging, and then they talk about food.

Larissa leans her chair back so that she can catch my eye behind my brother's back.

'My love,' she starts. 'How are you doing?'

I like that Larissa remembers to ask me that. That she cares. I'm about to answer when I'm interrupted.

'Nadia, why are you sour?' says my uncle.

'Problems at school?' echoes my mother.

'Better not be your grades,' counters Papa.

I look up.

Their conversation has already wandered onwards, to how bad school grades can ruin my future, and maybe I need tutoring, and doesn't Nastya who lives in Windsor have a brother named Vitya who owns a tutoring service?

We should call Nastya's brother Vitya at once, they decide.

This entire conversation occurs without me.

Distantly, I hear my uncle say that perhaps there is something wrong in my *private life*.

Private life is code for dating life. My blood starts to boil.

None of them bring up the fact that Lizzy is gone. That maybe my mood is sour because I recently watched my best friend die.

*

When someone you love dies, people give you about a month. In that month, if you cry, they know exactly why you are crying. But after that, whenever you're sad they ask you why. Expecting a different reason than the one before. As if your grief is past its expiry date.

As if your grief were a yoghurt.

I look up at them and I might as well be looking at a room full of strangers. Except my aunt Larissa, who shoots me a sympathetic look and rolls her eyes as if to say *what a bunch of idiots*. But that's not enough to soothe my anger. Nothing is. I'm seized with such hatred for everything, I feel my vision blurring.

'I was just thinking about Lizzy. It's her birthday.' My voice is less confident than I intended, a strangled croak. I know they are tired of hearing it but what am I supposed to do. Lie?

'You will be all right,' says my uncle.

'Just need some exercise, get your mind off things,' says Mama.

As if I could jog the thought of Lizzy away.

My grandmother adds more dumplings to my plate, even though I barely touched the first batch. I look up into her eyes, milky with age. That's all she can offer me, food. It's her medicine. She wants to fill the cracks in my soul with dough because it's the only way she knows how. I don't blame her. My anger eases a little bit as I look at her.

She was born right before the Second World War, and she grew up hungry. She lost her firstborn, Tomya. Many, if not most, of her friends are dead by now. Her husband is gone too. On her left hand she only has three fingers because when she was younger her neighbour slammed her door so hard in her face after an argument that she cut the other two clean off.

My grandma has been through a whole lot of pain, and maybe she's the only one who sees mine. But being seen doesn't feel like enough. Dough can't fill cracks this deep.

'You'll find another Lizzy,' my uncle says suddenly. And it's that particular sentence that brings me out of my stupor. I feel like a bucket of cold water has been dumped on my head. The conversation has moved on and circled back to my cousin's football career when I slam my hands down on the table.

'I CANNOT FIND ANOTHER LIZZY, YOU ABSOLUTE MORON!' I scream so loudly my voice cracks. Then I add a string of the dirtiest Russian swear words I can think of.

A cumulative gasp vacuums up the air in the dining room.

The whole table turns, almost slow motion; faces rotate and stop on me. Like they didn't even notice me there until this moment. It is uncommon to curse at your elders in our culture; I can feel my mother's shame bloom across the table. I'm in so much trouble.

Screw it. He deserved it. I'm so angry I could say it ten more times.

I realize that I'm standing. I realize that my hands are shaking. I can't breathe.

I have to get out of here.

I bolt out the door because I don't want to hear the reaction, or the scolding. Of course, it's still raining, and of course I'm not wearing my raincoat. I left it behind. I'll walk the whole way home. I welcome the iciness of the water. And I hope it gets me sick and I can miss school and spend a few days in bed watching *Gilmore Girls*.

Tears are quick to come; I don't bother wiping them because of the rain.

I don't really care who sees either.

I lost my best friend.

To my family, my sadness is well past its sell-by date and they're scared by my behaviour.

But my grief isn't a yoghurt, it's one of those American Twinkies I've read about online. It could outlive the Apocalypse. It could last for ever.

Sometimes I feel like it even could outlive *me*.

Hours later my family comes home. Papa walks by me, silently, carrying a sleeping Nikita to his room.

'You're in trouble,' says Stepa as he passes me. He's not gloating, it's a warning, a brother code. But he needn't have bothered since I already know cursing at my uncle is probably going to get me into a lot of trouble.

Mama returns my rain jacket and says she doesn't want to talk to me. Her blue eyes search mine, a flicker of worry passing across them, but it's quickly gone. She purses her lips. I dig into the pocket of my raincoat and I'm relieved that Lizzy's list is still there. There was a moment when I panicked and thought she might find it and throw it away.

'You upset your uncle, you disappointed me,' she says.

Them. Them. Them.

Mama sighs with dramatic exasperation and goes into the living room. I follow her.

Of course she wouldn't be on my side, even though

what my uncle said was horrible. How could he imply that Lizzy was replaceable? Why doesn't my own mother see the tears on my face, notice my red puffy eyes, sit down with me, comfort me?

She turns away from me and switches on Russian television, where some pop star is celebrating their seventy-fifth birthday on a stage. In Russia, once someone becomes famous, they never leave. Prime airtime is occupied by old barely mobile singers celebrating their birthdays and being showered with bouquets of carnations. It's super weird and ridiculous but it's more interesting to my mother than her own grieving daughter.

'Why go through the trouble of immigrating if you're going to pay a subscription every month just so you can watch some seniors celebrate their birthdays back home?' I say.

My mother turns to me. 'I've had enough of your attitude for one night.'

I've had enough of you, is what she doesn't say.

'Why don't you check the other channels, maybe someone is celebrating their centennial? Much more exciting than a seventy-fifth.'

'NADIA. You're about to get one on the brains!' she says in Russian. She's said this expression since I was little; it means I'm about to earn myself a slap. She rarely follows through on the threat. Though now her face is beetroot red and the vein in her neck is popping and I probably shouldn't push but I can't stop.

'Fine. I'll just go to my room. I don't want my emotions being an inconvenience when you've clearly got very important things to do with your life.' I eye the screen pointedly where they've just brought a clown onstage.

'That's it, you're grounded, or whatever it's called here.' She waves her hand in the air. 'No pocket money, no Wi-Fi. No outings with friends!'

'Lizzy was my only fucking friend.'

Mama falters for a second, but I don't know if it's because I've cursed, which I never do in front of her, or because of what I said. Tears sting my eyes and I dig my nails into my palms to stop them from coming. There's so much more I want to say to her. *You don't read my poems. You never hug me. If you made someone, aren't you supposed to be able to tell that they are breaking apart?*

'Not that you care,' I spit. 'You don't care about any-thing in my life. It's not as important as this week's deals on detergent.'

Her face goes red again; Mama reads the supermarket catalogues religiously. 'Go upstairs!' she screeches. 'You ungrateful brat. After everything that I do.'

I can no longer hold the tears, so I storm up the stairs. 'Enjoy your dumb programme,' I call down.

On the second-floor landing I come face to face with the open door to my parents' room. Papa is there, in his dirty worker overalls, sat on the perfectly made bed. His wrinkled face looks serious, clearly he has heard every word.

'Nadejda.' He says my full name. The word for *hope* in Russian. I stop and stare at him, my face aching from my desire to cry.

'I . . .' He struggles to find the words. 'I . . . knew it was Lizzy's seventeenth birthday.'

'And?'

'And that's it. I just wanted to say I remember. Sorry for not mentioning it earlier.' He scratches the back of his curly brown head. 'You should be nicer to your mama.'

There it is again. *You should be nicer.*

'Don't worry, Papa.' My voice is an empty husk, carved hollow with hate and a deep black anger. 'Dead girls don't have birthdays.'

Dad flinches; laughter trickles up from my mother's programme.

'Unlike pop stars,' I say. Then I head to my room.

CHAPTER 2

Is your herring in a fur coat fresh?

My grandma once told me that everyone in the Soviet Union wore grey, and that the busy morning pavements looked like flowing rivers of cement.

Well, the streets of my area at six on a Monday morning are like a literal interpretation of *Fifty Shades of Grey*. The buildings are grey, the sky is grey, the pavement is grey, even my polyester school uniform is grey. It's like the city has been leached of its colour.

There it goes again, that punch to the gut when something reminds me of her. Lizzy bought a copy of *Fifty Shades of Grey* at the supermarket last year and we did dramatic readings of it in the car park. Which made me laugh so hard I almost died by choking on a Jammie Dodger. The memory is like a screwdriver twisting into my stomach, tightening an already too-tight screw jammed there. I hate how my sad human brain makes me relive it all, again, again, and again. I think of something good, and then immediately there's pain. Immediately I feel the static of hospital bedsheets catching on my fingers and I see the outline of Lizzy's bony spine. I don't understand why my brain can't develop a defence mechanism to protect me from this.

My body has made an active effort to protect me from the life-threatening hazard that is pollen.

But it can't protect me from my grief.

I arrive at St Jude's, which is also grey. I walk down the linoleum hallway, keeping my head down. My classmates tend to give me a wide berth. Maybe they think my grief is contagious.

Marjorie, a girl whose only talent is being mean and so she resorts to it often, notices me. I don't know what her childhood damage is but I avoid her like the plague. I lower my head and keep walking. She sidesteps me.

'Hey, slagzilla,' she says as I stall in front of her. Her insults don't even make sense half the time. I've only had sex twice and both times were horrible. It was with a guy named Charles in the year above me. He was nice and fumbled and said *are you okay?* a lot but I was so desperate to feel something that I felt nothing at all. Lizzy was already in the hospital then. The excitement of talking about it with my best friend was still present, but over it hung a dark cloud – the weight of the different firsts she might never get to see.

So, calling me a slag, which is never justified anyway, also makes zero sense.

And I'm pretty sure Marjorie's never seen *Godzilla*.

Her friend and lackey, Josie, flanks her left. Josie has the personality of rice pudding. She belly-laughs at Marjorie's joke.

'Slagzilla,' she repeats, as if it might be wittier the second time around.

I've always ignored Marjorie, and when she said dumb mean things it was usually Lizzy who lost her temper with her. She always yelled back random stuff like *Shut up, you disgruntled mop*, and *Your face looks like a burnt scone!*

I was born round here, but Lizzy was born up north and her accent made everything sound cool. Lizzy was second-generation Russian like me, but she only moved south a few years ago down from the north when her mum got a fancy finance job in the city. I noticed her that first morning at school when I saw her backpack had a Soviet character on it. A big furry doe-eyed *Cheburashka*. I quoted the cartoon to her, and we were friends immediately.

Lizzy's accent stayed after her move. That was something I loved about her. The way she tamed language into her own unique expressions. One of the many things I loved about her. I swallow hard.

Marjorie wakes me from my thoughts by poking me.

'Did you not hear us, povvo?'

Great, now I'm a slag, a reptile and poor to boot. How original. I cock my head to one side and look at Marjorie coolly. Josie seems a little scared. Maybe it's my expression, which I've dubbed 'dead in the eyes resting bitch face'.

'Ugh, let's leave it,' she whispers and she tugs on Marjorie's sleeve. 'She's pathetic. Not worth our time.'

Marjorie considers this, but people have stopped. People are staring. And Marjorie likes an audience. She leans in.

'You know, I've been thinking.'

'That's unusual,' I fire back. At least I managed to get

a retort in this time. I'm quite pleased with myself.

Marjorie's eyes narrow.

'I've been thinking, being best friends with you, I'd probably drop dead from boredom as well.'

I know it's another dumb comment but this one cuts. Sometimes a fact buried inside a lie still is enough to hurt. *Lizzy died.*

All the other things she's ever said to me come back. *Slag. Giant nose. Estate rat.*

Marjorie fakes a yawn. 'Point proven, even trolling you is like watching paint dry.' Josie laughs. They turn, as if they could just walk away and leave all those words hanging in the space between us, stabbing out at me like birds in a feeding frenzy. Marjorie has a long braid that reaches down her back. I've never paid any attention to it, but now it's all I can see. I reach for it and I pull. And then I pull harder. It's all a blur but there are screams, and suddenly Marjorie is on the floor holding her head. I've dragged her a good few feet by her braid and then I swing. My fist connects with her cheek. Then I punch her a second time. Then I let the braid drop limply to the floor. I don't stop to process what I've done. I turn and walk away.

*

It's not really a surprise to anyone including myself that I am promptly called to the headteacher's office and suspended.

Mr. Harris stares at me over his desk. He pulls his glasses down the bridge of his nose, which seems unnecessary. I'm not sure why people do that, since they tend to give you this look like they can see you more clearly but really, they've just made you blurry. Behind him is a wall of all his successes. He's gone as far as framing his health and safety qualifications, which should give you an indication of what kind of a person he is.

He's asked me to call my parents so that's what I'm doing. Or pretending to do.

Instead I dial a local chip shop that I know never picks up and lets it ring to voicemail every single time. I know this because Lizzy and I used to leave them prank call voicemails. We imitated Liam Neeson's speech from *Taken*, only we pretended they had taken our cod. We sang the opening song from *The Lion King*. We once left a six-minute-long voicemail pretending to be the Kardashians.

There it goes, that familiar throb that rattles my chest.

Lizzy is never leaving prank calls again.

I speak into the receiver in Russian, repeating the phrase 'Is your herring in a fur coat fresh?' A phrase my mama always says at the Russian store.

Herring in a fur coat is a dish of layered pickled herring covered in mounds of boiled vegetables and eggs, soaked in mayonnaise and shaped like a cake. It's also a nuclear shade of purple, and I'm not sure it could ever be called *fresh*.

I say this phrase over and over again in different tones to pretend I'm asking my mum to pick me up, but my headteacher is none the wiser. He just nods along severely as if he understands and is in complete agreement with the herring being fresh. I conceal my amusement, realizing this is a prank Lizzy would have appreciated. Then I hang up the phone.

'They said they can't come get me, they have to prepare for a business trip tomorrow.'

Not sure what kind of business trip a plumber and housewife go on but I don't let Mr Harris catch on. I talk fast.

'And they said my aunt Larissa can come and pick me up and talk to you instead of them. But they are aware of the severity of the situation.' The head agrees and I call Larissa and beg her to come.

Mercifully, she doesn't ask any questions. Larissa

arrives half an hour later and she looks really good despite being a little wet from the rain.

She sits down, shakes her beautiful hair out.

'What seems to be the problem?' she says.

'Nadia here attacked a classmate,' says Mr Harris. He points at me, then corrects his hand so that he can pretend he wasn't pointing. He waits for a reaction.

Larissa turns to me. When she speaks her tone is kind. 'What did she say to you?'

Mr Harris scoffs; clearly he is not pleased with her reaction.

'We don't encourage violence, regardless of what words were exchanged!'

Larissa shoots him a terrifying look. 'I know my niece. I just want to know what was said to her to elicit such a reaction. She is not a violent girl.'

I shrug. 'She said maybe Lizzy dropped dead because of how boring I am.'

I hear their synchronized intake of breath.

'You didn't tell me this,' the head stutters. His gaze darts to Larissa as if he is mainly concerned with her opinion of him.

Larissa's blue eyes narrow predatorily.

'You didn't ask, you just suspended me,' I counter with

my best doe-eyed innocent gaze. I'm quite happy to throw him under the bus.

'Right.' Larissa picks up her fancy handbag. 'We will be going now. I'll call in tomorrow to see what disciplinary action has been taken against the other student as well. Since Nadia got a week-long suspension, it's only fair the other girl get a suspension for bullying. That's still an offence, is it not?'

'Yes, ugh, of course, naturally,' Mr. Harris stutters as we are halfway out the door. His gaze pauses on the divide between Larissa's black thigh-high boot and her mink coat. She makes it obvious that she noticed, then she saunters out.

'I hope you at least got a good one in,' says Larissa back in her car. 'What a cow!'

I think of Marjorie and how tightly my fingers had curled around her braid. Like I was about to play tug of war with it. She seemed so small when I knocked her down. I think about how Josie shrieked like a frightened hyena but didn't move to defend her friend. I feel a twinge of regret loop around my thoughts, and despite her bravado Larissa shoots me a quick and worried look.

Disturbed even. I've never lashed out at anyone physically before.

'I'm going to take you shopping,' she declares. My mouth opens and closes. That's not the reaction I was expecting.

We drive towards the shopping centre singing along to top hits on the radio. I don't sing as intensely as Larissa but I don't want to sit there silently like an oddball. When the new Shawn Next song comes on – '*Baby, you're right to be wrong*' – I cringe and turn the sound down. That same repetitive pain echoes through me.

Lizzy and I have matched Shawn Next's career beat for beat. We loved everything about him. And though we were always a couple of years behind in age we pretended we could relate to every lyric. When he was a doe-eyed and sweet teen, dressed in Easter-coloured polos with gelled-back hair, we launched ourselves into our preppy phase too. When he started using black eyeliner, we spent ages perfecting our tormented expressions and cutting the fingertips off of gloves for that perfect gothic look. We couldn't really afford to match Shawn's bougie clubbing era where he wore limited edition tracksuits, but Lizzy did beg her parents to take us to a posh sushi restaurant in London for her birthday. Ordering Yellowtail in an elite Soho restaurant on a Saturday night felt a little bit like being him.

Even though I've turned the music low I can still hear him. And my heart feels like it's tearing in half.

Right now, Shawn is in his acoustic era, close up mics and emotional songs about growing up famous. It's almost like our sad moments are synced too. But I can't wallow in his feelings any more, my own are far too strong.

I turn the radio off entirely.

'I thought you loved Shawn Next?'

I shrug. 'I used to.'

I used to love a lot of things.

'That's a shame, I think you've loved him since you were ten or something,' she says.

'Twelve,' I answer, almost automatically.

I remember the first time Shawn popped up on my TV. This blue-eyed, pink-cheeked boy that looked like an angel. He had his first hit, 'Coffee Shop Love', where he sat in a café looking all grown up, throwing lovesick glances at the waitress, who served coffee in a crop top for some reason. He was clearly too young for coffee, and the girl who played his love interest was about eighteen, but I fell for him hard. I got butterflies in my stomach and spent the night imagining what it would be like to kiss him, to be a waitress in his coffee shop. The next day in school Lizzy and I argued about who would get to be Shawn's girlfriend. Until we decided we'd share him. I'd get weekdays and she'd get weekends. Quite a complicated arrangement for a couple of tweens.

Pain rocks through me.

I wrap the memory up and put it on one of the shelves far back in my mind. The school counsellor told me to try and listen to some of the music Lizzy and I loved, but I just can't bring myself do it.

We pull into the grey lot of the shopping centre. It has a fancy name, like all shitty grey structures in the world do.

Larissa goes all out. She gets me some eyeshadow at MAC and buys me a set of make-up brushes. She gets me a leather-bound journal so that I can write more poetry. Then she buys me some *Friends* pyjamas, though I wish they had *Gilmore Girls* ones.

We steer clear of the Shawn Next section.

I like *Friends*. Even though it's about as dated as the birthday shows my mama watches, there is something incredibly comforting about a world where nothing horrible ever happens. I call it *the happy world*. You just know you won't switch on *Friends* one day and see Monica die while Rachel watches.

Sitcoms are hugs, and blankets, and hot chocolate.

Lizzy always joined me in that love. Even though she preferred *Star Wars* and fantasy fandoms and creatures with pointy ears and wings, she was always up for a *Gilmore Girls* marathon and hardly ever rolled her eyes when I cried over Jess.

Suddenly, I feel guilty that I didn't try as hard to like the things she liked.

I should have gone with her to Comic Con in London. I should have tried cosplay. Lizzy always tried to like the things I liked. And now she's gone and it's too late to ask her about it.

Larissa treats me to a caramel frappuccino at Starbucks, and we sit in her car slurping. I try to move my straw around in an effort to consume equal amounts of cream and caramel at the same time.

'What's going on in your head, love? I know it's about Lizzy, but talk to me,' says Larissa.

'I don't want to talk about it.'

I start to cry almost immediately. I sometimes don't

even get the warning, and my body just decides for me. Maybe there is too much pressure built up inside of me, and it only takes a tiny nudge for me to explode.

Larissa reaches for me and pulls me into a hug. I cry harder. Sobbing into her shoulder, probably drooling cream over her expensive sweater. I cry really *really* hard. Grateful that someone is there to witness it. Distantly, I wonder if I'm staying hydrated enough for all this crying that I do.

Larissa has been travelling for work and I've barely seen her since the funeral. Only at three family dinners, and never alone. Except for my outburst the other night she hasn't seen this side of me. She hasn't seen how broken I've become.

Larissa reacts differently to anyone else I know. She doesn't tell me to stop crying or to be strong, or that it will all be okay. She lets me feel. You would be surprised how many people want you to push your grief down.

Down. Down. Down. Where no one can see it.

Where they don't have to deal with it.

Maybe they are just worried the sadness will rub off on them, like wet paint on a park bench. I cry harder into Larissa's sweater, savouring being held like this. Being allowed to cry like this in someone's presence.

'I know it's not true. But I feel like I have nothing to live for,' I tell her.

'It's not true,' she echoes. 'I wish I could take some of the pain away, Nadush, but it will become smaller over time. I promise. It will shrink.'

Through snot I sob, 'And the worst part is I'm never going to complete her list.'

'What list, sweetheart?'

I reach into my coat pocket and retrieve the dirty off-white ball. Gently, Larissa unravels it like a Kinder egg. I watch her read it, half sobbing, half sipping my frap.

'She ...' Larissa struggles to verbalize what she's seeing. 'Lizzy wrote you a list of things to do after she died? To heal?' Larissa looks back at the list, running her finger over Lizzy's name.

'It's this thing, like a summer bucket list. We were going to do it together but once ...' I sob harder. 'Once she realized she wouldn't be there she rewrote it just for me.'

The crying starts to take on a life of its own. My shoulders shake and my breathing grows more erratic.

'She ... really ... loved *P.S. I Love You*. The film,' I explain, though I know it's more than that. She wanted me to get over it, and she thought this was the way. She cared about me even in death.

'But . . .' Larissa pauses, thinking. 'You can do some of these! Play bingo with old ladies? I can take you to the old Metro hall tonight!'

'No, it's all right. You've already done a lot. And I don't feel like it.'

Truth is, I don't feel like doing anything, and crossing things off that list just made me feel like Lizzy was deader than before.

'The godlike pop star, is that Shawn?' She points at another bit on the list and I nod. 'Then let me buy you a ticket to the next Shawn Next concert,' she offers. That's another point on the list. By far the most difficult item, it says *Get PJs signed by godlike pop star*. I don't know what Lizzy was thinking with that one. As if losing her wasn't hard enough, she also had to leave me an impossible to-do list.

'There won't be one anywhere nearby,' I explain. 'He had a bad experience at Heathrow last year and said he won't tour in England. He's touring the States right now but that's too far.'

Larissa thinks for a second. Then nods.

'You hungry?'

'Not really.'

'Look, I won't tell your mama and papa that you

got suspended. It's … it's not ideal. *But*, I don't think punishment is what you need right now.' Her eyes dart towards the list. 'It seems being in your head is punishment enough. If I can't make things better for you then at least I won't make them worse. I'm going to tell them I need you to stay with me for a while, and you can stay through your suspension.' She looks straight in front of her.

'Thank you,' I whisper through a sob.

'It's all right. I'm already the black sheep in the family, what can they do?' She laughs her wind-chime laugh and it makes me feel warm.

CHAPTER 3

Are you going to North Korea?

I'm in my room packing a small duffel to run off to Larissa's. Mama has been sulking since I told her. She walks by with the laundry hamper, stops and glares at me through the doorway.

'What exactly does she need your help with?' she tuts, then answers her own question. 'Cleaning out her garage full of designer clothes? Polishing her jewellery? Blow-drying her hair?'

'I get it, Mama, Larissa has a nice life,' I say, interrupting her rant.

'And doesn't she think I need your help here too? She is so selfish taking you away from me for a week.'

You're the one who is selfish. I bite back my reply. I'm her daughter, not an appliance; she should want me here because she loves me, not because she wants my help. For once I want to be worthy without being useful. I want to be useless and sad and wallow in it.

'You're just going to relax. I know it! Probably watch movies and go to the spa,' she says. 'And you will fall behind on your schoolwork. And Larissa doesn't know your bedtime.'

My bedtime? I'm seventeen, not seven.

I bite my lip and keep packing. There is little use in arguing with her and affecting my chances of going. I don't understand why she can't just be happy I'm invited somewhere after I've been so low lately. I've barely left the house in months – not since Lizzy got too ill for sleepovers.

We did get to spend a weekend alone by the seaside right after Lizzy's diagnosis. We ate fresh doughnuts, played penny pushers and skipped along the pier. Trying to pretend our world wasn't ending.

There should have been more trips. More sleepovers. More of everything. I stuff the last few T-shirts into my bag angrily. I bet if someone came up to me right now and offered me an all-expenses-paid trip to Disneyland, Mama wouldn't even be happy for me. *Couldn't* be happy for me. She would say that there are too many chores, and too much schoolwork. And why have fun when you can be productive?

Lizzy's family wasn't like mine; they let her have her freedom. I used to be so jealous of that. Of how her time belonged to her and just her, without having to be useful to someone. Without being dubbed a bad girl, or selfish, or lazy or ungrateful. Words used so much in my family they could go under our coat of arms. If we had one.

To me it felt like Lizzy had all the time in the world.

But then it ran out.

I say bye to my brothers. Nikita gives me a big squishy hug.

'I wish I was going to Aunt Larissa's,' he says. 'She probably has the best snacks.'

His curly hair smells like cherry dumplings as I bury my face in the top of his head.

'I'll bring you back something if you keep it a secret. Love you.'

'Love you,' he says and it ignites something in me. Stepa does an odd little shimmy, that's his way of saying goodbye. He mostly communicates in viral dance moves.

'I suppose a change of scenery could be good for you,' Mama says as I walk towards the door. She looks like she wants to say more but thinks better of it. The anger in me subsides a little as I search her eyes, desperate for more recognition. But she waves me off with a kitchen towel.

Larissa is outside waiting for me in the car. She's smart to not come in because Mama is giving her a death stare from the front door.

I settle in on the passenger side.

'Hey, Larissa.'

Larissa looks dead straight, it's almost kind of freaky. Then she speaks in a voice that sounds like that of a spy.

'Go back in the house and tell your mum you forgot something. Then sneak into her room, open her safe and take your passport. You know her combination, right?'

'What?'

Larissa's voice is urgent and it's freaking me out.

'You know her combination, right?'

I nod. The whole family knows it, in case of emergencies or World War Three or a zombie apocalypse (Stepa's theory).

'No questions, just do it. Now!' she hisses. I'm suddenly

worried that my aunt might be an ex-informant, and that she's making a break for it, and taking me with her.

No, Nadia, that doesn't make any sense.

'Now! Before your mama gets suspicious, oh and grab yours and Lizzy's pyjamas,' she urges.

Our pyjamas? I just gape at her. She's lost it. She has completely lost it.

I do as she says though.

I'm sitting on Larissa's couch and sipping some fancy tea full of bits of dried kiwi and strawberries and twigs or something. Our family only drinks black tea, nothing else. Everything in Larissa's house is different than in ours. Eclectic and bold and colourful, full of mementos from her travels. Silk scarves hung up on the walls, twinkly lights, fridge magnets with exotic city names.

I'm pretty sure Larissa spent most of her divorce money on travel, to my mum's great dissatisfaction. Every time Larissa would let us know that she couldn't make a Friday-night family dinner because she was jetting off somewhere new, my mama's face would scrunch up like a sea sponge and she would say that Larissa hadn't found happiness in her personal life yet. That was her snide way of saying that my aunt travelled because she was single. I think travelling sounds better than being in a relationship, but what do I know? I haven't really done either.

Larissa makes another cup of tea even though she hasn't finished her first one.

She has been acting weird since I got here. Pacing, muttering something to herself. She walks over and sits down facing me over the coffee table, which is littered with fashion magazines. Her gaze is intent.

In fact, she's being very intense and I set down my tea.

'I've done something,' she says.

This is the part where she tells me that she is a spy and then asks me to help hide the bodies.

'I booked a ticket,' Larissa says, her tone low as if someone might overhear.

Strange, Larissa has never been this intense about any upcoming travel. Usually, she just flippantly names the place and says *Ciao!* Where could she be going that requires this much secretive prelude?

'Are you going to North Korea?' I blurt out.

'What? No.' She shakes her head as if I'm being silly. 'I booked *you* a ticket to New York.'

'Why would I go to New York?'

That sounds stupid when I say it out loud. New York is

42

home to Beyoncé, it has hot dog carts and Times Square, there are one million and one reasons someone would go to New York. But why me?

'To see Shawn Next in concert and get your pyjamas signed,' Larissa says.

I'm lucky I put my tea down because I would have spilled hot water on my lady garden from the sheer shock.

Larissa doesn't wait for me to answer. She talks fast – nervously, like she's defending herself.

'This might be the worst most irresponsible thing I've ever done but I just can't stand to see you this unhappy. It's like you're fading. I'll tell your parents you need to stay with me till the end of the week and you will go for two days to New York.'

She hands me an envelope and I feel like I'm in one of those scenes in the movies where the main character pinches themselves to make sure they aren't dreaming. I *know* I'm not dreaming – but this doesn't feel like my reality either. I open the envelope. There is a printed booking for a return trip, Heathrow to JFK. There's also cash stuffed in an envelope, and a VIP ticket to the Shawn Next concert.

'I don't know how you will get close to him, that's up to you, but some people stay at the back entrance and wait.

Or you can try to find out his hotel and go there, I read online that people do that.'

When did Larissa have time to do all this? Or gather Shawn Next fan knowledge?

'How did . . .?' I can't even finish my sentence in this weird reality.

'I have the money,' she says as if that explains anything. 'And I have frequent-flyer miles for the flight. And it's not like you're a kid any more. You're nearly eighteen.'

I'm a number of months away from eighteen, but Larissa knows that.

'Mama will have a heart attack, she won't recover. She won't ever agree to a trip without adult supervision.'

'Exactly!' Larissa waves her hand in the air triumphantly. 'I thought of that. Your mama and I have a childhood friend named Vanya, he lives in New York and he's a cab driver. He owes me a favour and I called him, he agreed to pick you up at the airport and drop you back off, and he will be one phone call away for anything you might need the entire time. Obviously, your mama knows him so the whole thing is kind of supervised by a trusted adult.' She taps her temple. 'Genius, or what?'

I admit planning a concert, flight and semi-supervision in twenty-four hours is very impressive. I stare at the ticket in my hands, eyes widening. 'She still won't agree, not in a hundred years.'

'By the time she has a chance to disagree it will be too late,' Larissa says.

What does that even mean?

My aunt looks at me, her large eyes full of sadness.

'You need this, Nadia.'

CHAPTER 4

In true NYC fashion no one asks me what's wrong

Everything goes quickly after my first night at Larissa's. She lends me a few outfits, insisting I borrow her designer clothes so that I can look my best. She lends me a Gucci jacket that I think is worth more than my entire wardrobe. I have a distinct feeling that this is all a prank, or a test. That my mum will pop out of the wardrobe and say *Hah! I knew you would agree to go to America without telling me because you are an ungrateful, selfish child!* But that scenario seems less likely with each mile that brings me further from home and closer to the airport.

We are three hours early when Larissa parks her car in the car park.

She takes a deep breath and pulls out her phone, making sure to connect it to the car.

'We are going to call her now.'

'And if she says no?'

'Then you get on that plane regardless and let me deal with the consequences.'

Larissa presses the call button and I sink lower into my seat with each ring. Praying Mum doesn't answer promptly for once in her life. She's there on the third ring.

'*Da?*'

'Svetachka.' Larissa says her nickname like a coo and I can instantly tell my mum has gone rigid at the other end of the line.

'What do you want?' she says.

'Why do you assume I want something.'

'Because you always do.'

'*Pffft*, as if.' Larissa rolls her eyes. 'I have Nadia on speaker by the way.'

'She should be in school.'

'*Hmmm*, yes we will get to that. I need to talk to you about something. Something very important. Put Vassily on the phone too.'

The line changes slightly and my father says hello. I greet them both back and keep sinking. If I sink any further into my seat I will be on the floor mats.

'I want you to both listen to me,' Larissa says. 'Fully. And just let me talk for a second . . .'

An expectant silence expands on the line and anxiety gurgles in my stomach.

'As you know,' Larissa continues, 'Nadia has been very depressed since Lizzy's passing and she isn't getting any better. The time has come for drastic measures.'

'She doesn't—' my mother starts but Larissa cuts her off.

'*And* I have taken matters into my own hands. Lizzy left Nadia a list of things to do to try and . . . *heal*. And on that list is seeing Shawn Next in concert . . .'

Not long after Lizzy's death, I showed my mum the list. Hands shaking around the then still straight paper edges. She looked through it but all she did was complain about the points that related to boys. *There's no rush to do any of it, focus on your exams and you can do this someday later,* she added. Which I took to mean that there was no deadline. After all my friend was already gone.

My heart aches again now at those dismissive words.

At the ease with which she brushed off something my friend wanted on her deathbed.

I close my eyes and bite my lip as Larissa keeps going. She talks about the importance of closure, she tells them about their friend Vanya the cabbie and about all of the arrangements she's made.

When she's finished my mum's reply is instant. 'No, one hundred per cent no.'

Larissa looks angry. 'You won't even consider it, Sveta? Open your mind a tiny bit. It's not like she hasn't been on a trip before.'

'She has school.'

'I've called Mr Harris.' Larissa winks at me as if to say *It's just one little white lie in a sea of truths.* 'He's okayed two days of absence as long as she writes a report on New York, and Monday is a holiday. That's more than enough time for her to catch up on schoolwork.'

'No.'

My heart sinks into my stomach at my mum's word. The finality of it all. Even Larissa is starting to look nervous and deflated, despite having said I could just get on the plane if Mum said no. I don't think she was actually banking on going against my parents' wishes. She must have really believed she could convince her sister.

49

'Svetlana.' The frosty nature of my father's voice is about as cold as the tundra where he was raised as it cuts across the line. When his voice gets like that, conversations in our home come to a grinding halt. Even Stepa and Nikita will drop whatever they are doing. Especially if he uses any of our full names.

A moment later his voice is muffled, distant, but we can still hear him. 'Let her go, Sveta.'

My mother gets off the phone cursing at him in Russian. Papa hushes her. Then he's back on the line.

'Three days. Updates each day. Don't disappear,' my father says.

I'm too scared to move, too scared to speak and break this spell.

Larissa grins. 'She agrees, Vassily, thank you.'

'*S Bogom*,' he adds. *Go with God*. Then he hangs up.

Larissa and I stare at each other dumbfounded.

Larissa turns the car off, eyes still big with shock. Then she smiles wide. I return her smile.

'Never in a million years did I think that would work,' she admits.

'Me neither.'

*

I let Larissa help check me in. I'm in a daze the whole time.

They weigh my baggage. They tell me it's satisfactory. They give me a real boarding pass. They tell me a gate number. They wish me a good flight.

Larissa stills my hands when she sees them shaking. My fingers are curled around the boarding pass like a crab claw, as if someone would take the rectangular piece of paper away from me any minute.

My feet drag against the grey tiled floor of Terminal 5. 'Are you ... are you sure I should do this?'

'Am I sure you should go to New York for an awesome concert by your favourite singer? Hmmm ...' She pretends to think about it. 'Yes, I'm sure. Don't be such a chicken, Nadusha.'

Larissa treats me to a glass of prosecco at the terminal bar, to help 'calm my nerves'.

When we are done she practically pushes me towards the biometric gates.

'*S Bogom*.' She repeats the popular travelling mantra.

I look back at Larissa when I'm by security. She smiles. *It's not too late to run back*, I tell myself. But Lizzy's voice is there, loud in my head. As loud as it was when she would yell at me across charity shops when she had found something good. I used to shush her then, as bored shopkeeper eyes swivelled to our loudness, but I don't shush her now. I let the voice echo louder, basking in its presence.

Do it, the voice urges. So, I keep going.

Excitement and terror swirl into one in my stomach.

I wave at Larissa and smile back.

The seven-hour flight is the first time in a long time that I've been too distracted to think about Lizzy. The turbulence and snacks and the absolute silence that does not exist in my house disconnect me in the nicest, most calming way. Ten thousand metres up in the air is about as far away as you can be from your problems, and on this plane, I am unreachable.

The rest of the plane is dead asleep, soaking in the artificial darkness, and I don't know why they are wasting this precious on-board time.

I notice that the music section on my tiny screen includes Shawn Next's last album. My finger hovers over the button, but I'm not ready. Not yet. Besides, I will be hearing all of it at the concert.

I eat the free pretzels until I'm bursting and watch free movies till my eyes have that nailed-open feeling.

I fall asleep in the last forty minutes of flight time and wake up on the runway, completely disorientated. I've never been this far away on my own, never exchanged cash, or gone through immigration by myself, but after they stamp my passport it's pretty much a step-by-step process and my anxiety melts a little.

I search the faces and flowers of the arrival gate until I land on a stout man in a flat cap holding a sign that says NADEJDA.

Vanya has pink wind-chapped cheeks and I feel the callouses of his hands when he shakes mine.

'Parking is really expensive,' he tells me in Russian. 'Let's hurry.'

The cab stinks of leather and watermelon vape. Vanya drives fast, jerking in and out of spots and yelling at anyone who wrongs him. He tells me to call him Uncle Vanya, like the famous Chekhov play, and laughs at the joke he must tell often. He tells me a few facts about New York, and recommends I explore Central Park and get myself a lox bagel.

I quickly feel car sick, but I don't care because I can't stop staring out the window. We pass the largest cemetery I've ever seen.

'Did you know there are more dead people in Queens than there are living?' he tells me.

'No, I didn't. How, umm, interesting?'

The fact twists my stomach uncomfortably.

'My grandma is buried there,' he adds matter-of-factly. 'Not easy to get a spot, you know. Don Corleone is buried there too.'

I nod along, unsure of why Vanya is proud that his nan is buried alongside a famous mobster.

I don't hear what he says after that. I'm trying hard to suppress the images that come flooding into my head as I look at the seemingly endless graveyard.

The sound of dirt spattering against a coffin. White roses mixing with that dirt. People kept throwing flowers on her, on Lizzy, carnations and roses. As if she were a Russian pop star celebrating her birthday, not a corpse being lowered into the ground. I blink furiously, trying to push the images out.

Then *I see it*. The island. 'That's Manhattan,' Vanya says.

All shiny and chrome, it needs no introduction. I close my eyes tight and reopen them just to make sure it's real.

We cross the bridge and we're there. I have this weird urge to answer him in song. 'If you can make it here you can make it anywhere!' Instead I thank him for the ride, and the fun facts.

The whole city has a heavy air, as if it's steaming, like a sleeping dragon puffing little smoke-filled snores. Vanya pulls up next to a Travel City Inn. He hands me a plastic bag full of Tupperware.

'My wife Katya wanted to make sure you had food. Here's my card. WhatsApp me for anything you need. Absolutely anything. I'll be here to pick you up before your flight home. We wanted you to stay with us, you know, but Larissa said Brighton Beach is too far from the concert.'

'Thank you, thank you so much for everything,' I say, lamely clutching the bag of Tupperware to my chest.

'Of course,' he huffs. 'Anything for Larissa. Wash *those*,' he adds pointing at the Tupperware. 'Katya loves her Tupperware.'

I nod and make a mental note to ask Larissa what she did for Vanya that was so special.

He drives off and I stand on the bustling pavement staring up at the building. I'm suddenly seized with an irrational fear that the clerk won't check in a seventeen-year-old, but they couldn't care less, way more interested in flirting with the other clerk than paying attention to me.

My room looks like probably any other room in any Travel City Inn in the world. I've been to one in Surrey when my dad took me to a plumbing supply conference (not the most thrilling weekend of my life – never had I ever thought I could sit through an hour-long presentation on pipes).

But this Travel City Inn isn't like every other Travel City Inn in the world because I can see all of Manhattan from my window. It's beautiful and glorious but I'm also a little afraid of it. I'm ashamed to say I'm so afraid of it that I don't go out for dinner. I just stay in, kind of telling myself that it makes perfect sense that I'm in NYC and that I won't venture out for dinner. Because I need to save the money, and because I need an early night, and because the concert is tomorrow. But mainly I'm too afraid of what's behind my door. The Travel City Inn is something I know, everything beyond that is frightening.

I snack on the crisps I have left over from the flight and I drink tap water because I'm not sure the conspicuous water bottles on my nightstand are free. Then I eat all the food Katya packed for me cold. I know I complain about my culture but the fact that a stranger would drive to pick me up, and his wife would worry about what I eat for dinner, is the nice bit about being Eastern European.

I scribble a few notes in my poetry journal. Trying on a poem about New York and how it's all concrete and steaming. I feel like a fraud though because I have no business writing about a city I don't even have the nerve to go and explore.

The last thing I do is iron mine and Lizzy's Shawn Next PJs. I want them to be crisp and straight when I meet him, when I get them signed. That's what Lizzy would have wanted. I ask the lobby for some cardboard and a marker and I pen a sign: MY BEST FRIEND'S LAST WISH WAS FOR YOU TO SIGN HER PJS. It's a cheap shot but I spent half the flight pondering how I could get noticed by Shawn when I'm one of thousands who want him to see them.

With Larissa's ticket I will be close to the stage and he's bound to read it. Visions of Shawn inviting me up onstage and signing the PJs in front of hundreds of thousands of crying fans fills my brain. But I try to not get ahead of myself.

I fold the cardboard up as small as I can get it, in case security doesn't like people bringing in signs. Then I tuck it into a tote bag.

*

You know that feeling when you're so nervous that you wake up way before your alarm? Or maybe it's the jet lag. But whatever it is I'm wide awake and buzzing at four in the morning and it's still dark outside. For a while, I just watch the city from my window. I watch it wake up, not that it ever really slept. But progressively the tiny people like singular ants twenty or so floors below me turn into a buzzing colony. The streets grow packed. Again, the city starts to steam – trucks, hot dog vendors, doors swinging and letting out the heat.

It takes me a while to gather up the courage to go down to breakfast.

'Do you want the last muffin?' someone asks me and I startle so much that I release a small yelp.

'I didn't do anything,' I say. 'I mean, huh?'

A girl close to my age stares at the buffet in front of us. Pointing her metal tongs at the last muffin. She has bouncy blonde hair and a button nose. 'I said, do you want the last muffin?'

'Oh, no I don't,' I lie. I'm so embarrassed that I startled like a caged hyena. Suddenly, I notice the girl is wearing a Shawn's Nest T-shirt.

'You a birdie?' I point at the T-shirt. She smiles the toothiest smile I've ever seen.

That's what Shawn Next mega-fans call themselves, because they are baby birds in Shawn's Nest. Tweeting and chirping about all things Shawn. It's adorable, or lame, depending on who you ask. (Stepa would tell you it's super lame.)

'The biggest,' she gushes. 'Savannah, come over here. She's a birdie too.'

Her brunette friend joins us and we stand in a short silence. 'Are you here for the concert?' she asks.

'I am. You guys?'

The first girl nods vigorously. 'Yup. Drove all the way from St. Louis through the night. Took turns though.'

St. Louis. Something about the city jogs my memory. There was an old film I saw with my nan . . . No it's not that. Then suddenly I remember a Shawn Next biography Lizzy got me for Christmas. It was a heavy glossy thing with sharp corners, one of my favourite gifts.

'St. Louis. Isn't that where Shawn is from?'

Savannah beams. 'Yup, and his parents still live there.' She smiles wide as if that somehow deepens her connection to the singer.

'I'm Ashley by the way,' the blonde muffin poacher says. 'Are you excited for the concert? Is it your first?'

'My name is Nadia and yeah. My aunt gifted me tickets.'

'Nadia,' Savannah repeats. Trying the name on for size.

I don't tell them the rest of the story. No one needs to hear about death first thing in the morning.

'Is it *your* first Shawn concert?' I ask out of politeness. I already know the answer. Both girls are wearing official concert merch T-shirts.

'Oh my gosh no. He was so good when I saw him in Atlanta, and really good in Boston, but, like, way better in New York last year.' Ashley gestures a lot when she talks, and I bet her and her friend are the popular ones at school. Maybe even on the cheerleading team.

Suddenly I find her irritating. How many Shawn Next concerts does one person need?

'Have you ever met him?' she asks me.

Okay, now I *really* hate her.

'No,' I say sullenly. I already know why she's asking.

'We did last night,' Savannah gushes, nearly squealing. 'First time *it* worked.'

I wait for them to tell me what the 'it' is.

'We, like, waited for four hours by his hotel,' Ashley explains. 'Finally got my autograph and a selfie.' She pulls out her phone and shows me. I fake a smile. 'He, like, was so freaking nice. You wouldn't believe it. Even said my name out loud. This was my eighth time waiting at one of his hotels but if you try hard enough you get there in the end. You know?'

I've never met real-life groupies before. It's kind of fascinating.

'So, do you think if I wait at his hotel today,' I force myself to ask, 'I could meet him?'

'I mean not now, they were upset enough we found him last night,' says Savannah.

I nod. Feeling a little sorry for Shawn suddenly. It's a little bit like having a target on your back. Everyone wants to get close enough to see you, but no one can truly get close enough to know you.

'Who's they?' I ask.

Ashley rolls her eyes. 'His management. Very protective of his whereabouts.'

'How *did* you guys find him anyway?'

'There's a thread of his leaked locations. I can send it to you, give me your number.' I hand over my phone and she puts her number in with a smiley face next to it.

'Text me.' She smiles. 'We are off to Madame Tussauds.' Both girls wave at me.

Her phrase lingers with me. *If you try hard enough you get there in the end.*

I eat my now cold scrambled eggs and toast alone, letting it settle in my displeased stomach – a stomach that expected lunch but got breakfast. I finish up and finally muster the nerve to go and explore. I know exploring an awesome foreign city shouldn't take nerve, but my body fights me on it. A small voice in my head tells me that I could go back to the safety of my room and draw the blinds. I could get under the covers. Nothing bad can happen under the sheets. But I tell that voice to go, the way Lizzy would.

I already let Larissa know I landed using airport Wi-Fi, and later that I had checked in.

> I'm off to explore New York. (Cue Alicia Keys). Have I told you you are the best aunt in the world?

I hold the phone up to the skyline view in my window and record another voice message for my dad, stuttering over my words as if I'm somehow in trouble. I let him know I'm safe and going to do some sightseeing. Dad answers back with a simple acknowledgement of receipt. But there's nothing from my mum. I doubt she will speak to me till graduation.

Before heading out I shut my phone off, terrified I might accidentally switch on my roaming.

The streets are full to bursting and I think people get irritated with me because I linger at the lights, I hesitate before turning. I try to figure out where I'm going and that takes time. New Yorkers don't like the rhythm of their streets being disrupted, especially by wide-eyed tourists like me. I've learned that much from films.

I visit Central Park. I walk all the way up to John Lennon's Strawberry Fields. My brother Stepa, the music buff, would love this.

I traverse the park back to the Upper East Side. People there look really rich, and they have buggies that look like they're from the future. I buy a hot dog and sit on the Met steps and eat my lunch there as if I were a character on a TV show. I start thinking about how Lizzy will never see the Met, or Central Park, or have a New York hot dog. And then I cut those thoughts off at the root. Grief has made me a gardener in my own mind. I'm always pulling at roots, cutting off stems, hacking down parasitic thoughts that threaten to overgrow me.

A little while later, I stand in the middle of Times Square, letting neon lights and the movement of the commercials wash over me. I cry a tiny bit and I move to hide it but then I realize no one cares. No one looks at me. New York is a wave and it will crash over you, one way or another, it doesn't stop to talk. You're unseen in New York – unheard – and you can get lost and disappear. I can see why some people would hate that but to me it feels like the best thing ever.

I walk down Broadway and look at the shows and their sparkly banners. I imagine being able to see *Hamilton*, to just rock up and get tickets to anything you want. Somehow my grief has made me think way more about the things I don't have. Maybe no longer having a best friend has made me realize I don't have a lot of other things that I want either. And realizing the world is unfair makes me think I may never get those things. One thing I know for sure is that my self-pity feels a little bit better than the sadness. But it eats away at you. You can't feel whole when you are feeling sorry for yourself.

*

I ride the subway. It's dirty and I get lost, so I exit and walk the fifteen blocks back to the Travel City Inn. Back in the safety of my room I study the subway map so that I know exactly how to get to Madison Square Garden for the Shawn Next concert. Tucking my passport and half my money in the safe, I pack my bag and send Larissa another check-in.

I sit there with my make-up all done and wearing a fancy green silk dress I borrowed from my aunt. It's designer and I keep straightening it out over my body as if my skin would instantly wrinkle it. Then I kill time by going over Lizzy's list because, apparently, I like to suffer.

My thumb runs across the final point on list. *Visit my parents.* This is probably the one I feel most guilty about not completing. Lizzy's parents only live ten minutes away from me. I should have visited them a long time ago. I've tried, but I can't. I'm ashamed to admit that I've not visited them since the funeral. But I can't help myself – their house feels like a tomb. And their eyes feel like graves; they hold sorrow and death and hollowness. Lizzy was their only kid and their pain isn't something I can quantify. What possible comfort could I offer them if I can't even comfort myself? I wonder if they hate me for never visiting.

My eyes linger on number 8 – *Get PJs signed by godlike pop star.*

I never talk to Lizzy in my head or out loud, even though the school therapist said I should and that it would help. But I feel like an idiot talking to an empty room. The few times I did try it I got really angry – so angry that she couldn't talk back to me.

But I try it now, because this is a special occasion.

'Lizzy.' My voice breaks instantly, as if her name were a jagged rock. 'I'm about to try and get our PJs signed by Shawn. I'll tell him you said hi.'

That's about as far as I get before I have to stop and the tears pool. My rage is blinding and hot because the hotel walls do not answer me. My mascara burns like hell. I fix my make-up, grab my stuff and stalk out the door.

I'm on the subway and I've studied the route a number of times. Left plenty of extra time for delays. I don't talk to anybody, just people-watch. The movement of the train is throwing me around and I hold on to the metal pole for dear life.

A cute boy by the doors keeps throwing glances my way and my cheeks get hot. He's wearing ripped acid jeans slung low around his hips and an oversized threadbare hoodie. Everything about him screams *big city*. The train jerks violently and he falls forward a little, knocking right into me. He instantly skips back looking mortified.

'Sorry about that,' he says. He says it in the proper accent of a New Yorker. I nod but don't manage to actually say anything back. He shoots me a shy smile and I can feel his touch where his hands were on my arm. It's a little weird. He brushes his long blond curly hair out of his face. Gives me one last sheepish grin. The doors open and he leaves.

'See ya,' he calls with the wink of a campaign model.

'Laters,' I say but he's gone. And thank God because what kind of loser says *laters*? I'm pretty sure I've never said that before in my life.

My stomach does a somersault and I want to do that shriek-swoon sound that I used to make when I would watch new Shawn Next videos. I should have said something to the cute guy, Lizzy would definitely have said something cool. Jesus, why am I such a coward? I should have told him my name. Or my socials.

I'm still thinking about the boy when someone taps me on the shoulder.

67

'Excuse me,' says an older man in a pea coat. For a moment I'm scared he might flash me, but then he points behind me. 'Your bag is open.'

I don't understand the meaning of his words at first. Then I look at my bag.

'Oh! Sorry, thank you so much, sorry,' I say in the most British way possible. I turn to close my bag but the way that it gapes at me, like an open mouth, startles me. Realization whips into my head like a car crash. The lip of the handbag Larissa lent me is open. Why would my bag be open? I remember closing it.

My wallet's gone – and the Shawn Next ticket was in it!

I stumble forward as the train shakes.

'The boy,' I say to no one in particular. *The cute boy with the long hair.* 'He took it!'

He must have reached into my bag when he fell against me. The older man gives me a sympathetic look but then turns back to his paper. No one in the carriage looks up as I burst into tears.

I feel violated and stupid and naive.

Suddenly, I'm so full of anger. That asshole can't just take my stuff and get away with it! I exit at the next station and pelt up the steps.

I run up to train security.

'Excuse me.' I knock on the glass. 'I've been robbed.'

The woman looks up at me, her expression lazy and bored. Her brown eyes narrow. 'At gunpoint?'

'What? No.'

'Knifepoint?'

'Jesus, no, this boy stole my wallet, from my bag, he was blond, blue eyes, and—'

'Oh, you mean you've been pickpocketed,' she cuts me off.

Really?

'Sure, whatever you want to call it. He took my wallet. If you hurry and walkie-talkie it in or something. They might still catch him.' I look at her expectantly.

The woman tips her chin to the ceiling and roars with laughter. Her laugh is loud and unnecessarily long. 'You want me to *walkie-talkie it in*?'

I stare at her dumbfounded. Eventually, she stops laughing.

'Describe the thief please,' she says, turning serious once she's realized I'm not kidding. There is still a bemused smile on her lips as she jots something down in her notebook even though I haven't told her any-thing yet.

I recall every detail of the boy's face while she

continues to give me a bored look. The woman scribbles a few more notes, then puts the paperwork aside.

'Are you going to try and find him?' I ask. I stare vacantly at the greasy fingerprints I've left on her glass. 'There was important stuff in that wallet.'

'Honey.' The woman tucks her pen away and looks at me with pity. 'We are never ever going to find him. Do you understand? I'm sorry. Do you have any idea how many people get pickpocketed on the New York subway?'

I want to scream at her. I want to bash my hand against the dull glass.

None of this is her fault though.

I leave her my Travel City Inn contact details 'in case my wallet shows up'. We both know it's a joke.

I take the train back to the station where the boy first exited. I run around frantically looking for him even though a part of me knows he's long gone. Probably to the Shawn Next concert.

A vengeful plan forms in my head. I will go to Madison Square Garden and wait for him, to intercept him.

But there are probably dozens of entrances and my plan is stupid. I've already wasted so much time.

I crumble on a platform bench and start crying again. And again, no one asks me what's wrong.

I wish they would this time.

I would tell them that I lost my Shawn Next ticket and that I will never complete Lizzy's list.

And that I have absolutely no one to blame but myself.

The next morning my whole face hurts from crying. I've cried a lot since Lizzy died, but never as hard as yesterday. My throat is raw from the sobs, my eyes are sticky and swollen. I splash my face with cold water, trying to bring down the swelling.

My nostrils are also dry and chapped from blowing my nose with the cheap toilet paper so many times. My legs hurt from all the standing and walking.

I waited at Shawn's hotel for six hours. I found the thread that Savannah and Ashley from the hotel had recommended, then I walked uptown and waited there. First in the lobby, then outside when I got busted. Then huddled on the kerb when the cold seeped too deep into my bones. Eventually I went home. I cried myself to sleep long after I knew the concert was over and the fans would be on their way home, singing 'Broken-hearted Girl', and clutching their souvenir tickets and fading glow stick jewellery. Long after I texted Larissa that the concert was amazing, that everything had gone to plan. Delaying the inevitable truth by at least a day. I will have to tell her everything when my flight lands.

There's another seven hours before Vanya picks me up. I'm meant to check out and explore until my evening flight. That's enough time for me to get my crap together, I tell myself. The last thing I want is to cry in his cab. I zip up my suitcase and throw my makeshift sign into the bin. Flinching as my eyes catch on the text. The tears come back. I'm not sure they will ever stop.

It wouldn't be the first time I've cried to a cab driver anyway. A few weeks after Lizzy died, I got far too drunk at a party. Someone called me an Uber and I demanded the poor driver take me to the castle swans, down by the river where Lizzy and I used to feed them.

We joked about catching one and cooking it. We would never do that, but killing swans is treason in England and so it's fun to talk about.

Lizzy would climb up on an ancient-looking wall and perform a clumsy *Swan Lake*.

We fed those infernal birds, beautiful and nasty, watched their grey matted babies stumble into the cold water for the first time then float gracefully like dandelion clocks. All best friends have that special thing they do; a thing that's so simple, like feeding swans, but is magical because you're doing it with your best friend.

I haven't fed the swans since.

That drunken night I looked for the swans, swaying clumsily. Turns out swans also sleep and are nowhere to be seen at night. I cried the whole way home. I even cried into the petrol station sandwich that nice Uber man bought me, then I threw it up in Mama's rosebushes.

The memory makes me hot and nauseous as I ride the lift down for breakfast. I look for an empty table and settle in. Unable to stomach more than a few nibbles of my muffin.

Larissa's beautiful face flashes before my eyes. I think of what she's done for me and how I screwed it all up. How am I going to face her and tell her I messed up her generous gift to me? Maybe I should just sign the pyjamas myself and pretend I succeeded? Put on a brave face for her?

No. She'll see right through it.

I failed. I'm miserable. I'm an embarrassment.

I wish I were dead.

A trail of giggles pulls me from my dark hole. The Shawn Next girls have arrived for breakfast. Giggling in what is undoubtedly a post-concert euphoria. I can't believe they got to meet Shawn. They don't even need it like I do. The girl's phrase from yesterday lingers on the edge of my mind.

If you try hard enough you get there in the end.

Suddenly, I have a massive shift of feeling, which frankly happens a lot when you're grieving. One minute you're devastated, the next minute you're completely numb, and before you know it you're overcome with the deepest rage you've ever felt. I know people say grief goes in linear stages, but I feel like it zigzags back and forth from one stage to the next and back again.

Like it's a heart rate.

I check Shawn Next's Twitter but there's nothing except a tweet thanking his fans for the concert and saying he's excited to see his parents.

His parents who live in St. Louis.

The fan's words are still ringing in my brain.

If you try hard enough you get there in the end. I deposit my dirty plates on a pick-up tray, but I don't go upstairs, I don't head outside, instead I approach the table of tittering girls.

Their faces pivot up at me.

I smile, and it feels a little too haunted. A little too hopeful. 'How would you like to make some money?' I say.

CHAPTER 5

Meet him in St. Louis

It's early the next morning. I've fallen asleep somewhere between strip malls and unfamiliar county lines. Savannah and Ashley have taken shifts driving, with breaks for iced lattes and to sleep at a rest stop in the middle of the night.

What the hell am I doing here? The realization is stark and sobering as we pass a sign that says we are close to St. Louis. *Have I lost my mind?*

It was a fourteen-hour drive in total and I'm not sure exactly at which point I drifted off.

The dashboard in the car tells me my flight home

landed a while ago. Nervously, I squeeze my phone in my palm.

I managed to convince Vanya that I was bored and had gone ahead to the airport. A few hours into the flight time I sent Larissa an email that would make sure she wouldn't be at the airport waiting for me. I click on the email icon and re-read it for a fifth time.

> Larissa, there's something else I need to do in America, I'm not done with Lizzy's list. I know this will sound crazy but I just need one more day. I will take a Sunday red-eye and be back Monday. I'm sorry this will probably worry you, and I feel like a trash niece, but don't worry, I'm safe, I haven't been kidnapped. There's just something that I really need to do . . . P.S. PLEASE PLEASE PLEASE DON'T TELL MAMA. If there's any way you can stall till Monday. I love you.

I'm aware my email will make her heart jump right out of her chest but I had no choice. I *had* to let her know I wasn't coming back yet so she wouldn't go and pick me up, and that I was safe so she wouldn't call the police, but couldn't quite bring myself to call her and tell her why. And now I'm starting to feel like I've made a huge mistake.

I crack my neck and stretch my fingers out as Savannah lectures Ashley on some Netflix show I'm not familiar with. My hands are tired from all the sleuthing I've done.

In-between sleep, I spent most of the drive mooching off Savannah's internet and combing through the decade-long Reddit thread on Shawn Next. Then I skimmed his biography, which I got at Barnes and Noble on one of our evening stops. I study the St. Louis chapters, learning he grew up there, riding BMX bikes with his best friend, and that he lived on a quiet street in a suburb.

Not much to go on.

I've managed to find Shawn Next's family address on an old buried thread. I google the address and find that his parents' house is also marked on a 'Map of the Stars' map for a 'Celebrities bus tour' that focuses on the homes of country singers mostly. I try and sleep a little more. As if sleep could make me forget what I've done. Or less scared of what I'm about to do.

I ask Savannah to drop me off at the bus stop and give her 150 dollars for gas.

'Look me up if you're ever in London,' I say. Even though I don't really mean it.

Both girls look happy to be rid of me. I didn't tell them about my plans because frankly I don't want them to join me. To them I'm just some weirdo trying to get to St. Louis.

I take the tour and snooze through the country star homes and the home of some B-list drummer. I perk all the way up when they announce Shawn Next's house, craning my neck like a nosy giraffe.

It doesn't look very impressive. It's a white house with a white picket fence and slightly worn shutters. Large but not notable.

I wait till we are at the next house, where some guitar rock legend used to live, and throw parties that included baby raccoons for some wild reason.

I tell the driver that I have cramps. He pulls over and lets me get off the tour bus, no questions asked.

I trace back the ten or so blocks it takes to get back to the white house with the white picket fence.

I'm pretty proud of my spy skills to be honest, and if MI6 have not yet recruited Larissa perhaps they should give me a crack.

Nadejda Vasilieva – locator of the stars.

My footsteps slow involuntarily when I get close to the house. *Oh my God this was a bad idea.*

What the hell am I going to say?

First, I will ring the buzzer, apologize profusely for the inconvenience and then explain everything to them. *Or him.* OH MY GOD SHAWN NEXT MIGHT OPEN THE DOOR. Then I will properly freak out. *No.* Stay calm, Nadia. If his parents open the door you tell them about the concert and Lizzy and then ask them for help getting your PJs signed. And maybe Shawn Next is going to open the door and I'll tell him everything.

I'm going to lose my breakfast.

My scenarios seem less likely the closer I get to the door. I knock. Once, twice ... nothing. I almost feel relieved. I force myself to knock a few more times for good measure. Still nothing. Panic starts to creep in.

'Hey you!' someone hollers. I startle and whip around.

There's a boy standing in the driveway next to me, a rubbish bag in hand.

'What the hell do you think you're doing?'

His voice is deeper than I expected a guy around my age to have, his accent local.

He drops the rubbish bag and crosses the immaculate lawn until he is facing me. I'm seized with the desire to run but I hold my ground. I haven't done anything wrong. Not really.

Up close I take him in and something in my chest hitches. He has tanned skin and wavy dark brown hair falling into his equally dark eyes. He runs his hand through it and I notice it's slightly damp from the beating sun. His gaze settles on me, and I find myself unable to speak. I'd tell myself it's just nerves, because he looks like he's going to shout at me, but it's also because he's hot. Well, he would be if he didn't look so outraged. Is he outraged by ... *me*? His scowl deepens, making the fluttering in my stomach turn into a hurricane. He closes the distance between us, forcing me to look up, straight into those bronze eyes. I realize I'm cowering so force myself to straighten up and look him right in the eye.

'What do you think you're doing?' he demands.

'I just—' I start but he cuts me off.

'You just what? Thought you could come and harass people at their homes. You're another Shawn Next fan, aren't you?'

I want to deny it but why else would I be standing here? He looks pointedly at the Shawn Next biography still in my hands. Oh my God, I'm mortified.

'You are!' he declares. He points at the door. 'These

80

people deserve privacy, you know. Do you even understand that they are *real* people?'

'You're really aggressive,' I say weakly.

Tears are pricking my eyes and I blink until they go away. I'm not going to break down and cry in front of a stranger – especially not an angry hot one that's making my stomach churn.

He'll think I'm having a super-fan tantrum.

'I'm the aggressive one?' He looks genuinely shocked. A muscle ticks in his jaw. 'You're the one stalking someone, coming to someone's home uninvited, now that's aggressive!'

It's too late – the tears have arrived. Briskly I turn and walk off down the slanted driveway, furious. He calls after me but I don't stop. The tears are hot and I'll be damned if he sees me melt into a puddle. I keep walking and walking. By the time I turn the corner a sob escapes me and I'm so glad I got away. The sun is hot on my face and the houses are very large and very white. I feel out of place. I feel like a stain on a white tablecloth.

This neighbourhood is like something out of a film, one of the houses even has a swing tyre out front. It probably has a TV room as well, and a kitchen island and pool table. Everything is so much bigger in America.

I walk for a whole twenty minutes till I hit a proper street that has anything except a row of large houses on it. I go to a Starbucks. It's big and noisy and I get one of those frothy iced mochas covered in whipped cream and doused in caramel. I sit on a stool facing the window so that no one can see me cry. I hear the clang of laptop keys, and the cheerful shouting of names, and it's funny how you travel to the other side of the globe and find yourself in a Starbucks that is exactly like the one back home. The world is different, but it's still connected by identical Starbucks.

That boy was an asshole but he was right. It's ridiculous what I'm doing. I've lost my mind. I can't just stalk Shawn Next's parents. I have to go home. I'm supposed to be back in my house. I'm supposed to be suspended.

I don't know where to go. I'm going to have to figure out a way to get a ticket home. I have some savings and I hope that covers whatever a last-minute ticket costs. I'll just get a cheap one-way and maybe Larissa has managed to keep my little detour secret for one day. I doubt it. My phone is an itch at the bottom of my pocket but I tell myself I will check her reply when I'm at the airport. When I actually have a solution to my temporary madness.

I wander around looking for a bus station and when I find one I see that the next bus is in two hours because it's a freaking Sunday and I'm kind of in the middle of nowhere. Getting a taxi seems like a good idea to eat away at a chunk of my money. Hitch-hiking seems like a really bad idea. Or like a really good way to get killed.

I've seen American horror films. Hitch-hiking in America is less cute than it is in Europe.

One summer Lizzy came back from visiting France with her family with the novel idea that if we couldn't afford to take the train to London on the weekend we could simply write LONDON on a piece of cardboard and stand by the roadside until someone deigned to take us.

'It's all the rage in Europe,' she announced. Gingerly writing the word MILAN on a decapitated cereal box. 'You can get anywhere you want, for free.'

We planned to travel around Europe with backpacks the following summer, writing out our next destinations on the backs of the cereals that sustained us.

I blink the memory away. Hitch-hiking sounds less *ooh la la* and more like the start of a true crime episode.

I'm going to have to get back to the airport on the bus. Then stay at a hotel if there are no red-eyes on a Sunday night and then use all of my savings for a new ticket for Monday morning.

I hate that I betrayed Larissa in this way. She trusted me. She gave me a chance and I ruined it. I'm crying again. Then my stomach rumbles in protest and eventually I'm too hungry to cry.

I'm drawn by the pink-and-green neon of a diner across the massive four-lane road. Also, I've never been to a diner and it seems like the most quintessentially American thing to do. I could order a strawberry milkshake.

I walk in shyly, mesmerized by the neon signage and the metal counter-top that stretches and curves along the side of the restaurant like a silver river. There's a jukebox too, and an old gumball machine. Everything is chequered and white and red and a large statue of Elvis presides over a booth in the corner. There are old rusty Coca-Cola signs and a portrait of James Dean.

The smell of waffles and coffee is strong despite it being evening.

Two people by the bar have baseball caps on and are watching a football game on the TV. I ease into a red booth and a waitress appears.

'Whatchagonnahavehoney?' she asks me, as if it's all one word.

I order a cheeseburger and fries and vanilla malt milkshake, then I order a slice of cherry pie from the revolving glass cabinet. The waitress calls me *honey* again and looks at me a little weirdly when she hears me speak. The food arrives very quickly and I eat, pretending I'm studying the large flappy plastic menu so that I can avoid eye contact with everyone.

The menu is kind of weird actually. Who wants chicken-fried steak covered in gravy, with a side of fries and steak sauce? Or eggs topped with onion rings and chilli?

I'm eating my burger and feel that familiar burning in my eyes. Tears, again. OH, MY FREAKING GOD. I can't even tell you how tired I am of crying! For one, there is a physical toll. It hurts and your eyes get achy and sore from all that muscle work. Your skin feels raw, rubbed, and you get these tension headaches in-between your brows. I just feel sad because I failed, again. I'm not sure why Lizzy ever thought I could do this list thing. I'm a coward and I'm weak. Maybe she regretted being friends with me towards the end. She could have lived more fully if I wasn't holding her back. If I wasn't sticking to my training wheels.

She could have gone full speed.

I know my thoughts have turned down a bad path

because my cheeks are wet, the sting is gone, the tension relieved, but fat blobs are streaming down my face. And soon comes the sniffling, and I'm holding back those deep body-rocking sobs that come next.

Through the wetness of my lashes I spot someone blow through the swinging doors.

Oh no, no no no. The boy who yelled at me earlier comes into the diner. I tuck my head behind a menu and sag in my booth. He can't see me here, crying. He will think I went straight to the local diner to weep over not getting into Shawn Next's house. How pathetic! I don't know why I care what this boy thinks. But I kind of feel transparent in front of him. I'm praying he orders a burger to go and leaves but I risk a glance from behind the menu and shit! *Shit, shit, shit, shit.*

He's gone behind the bar and he's pulling a tattered apron on and tying it behind his back. I watch him wipe the counter, his tanned arms flexing with each movement and making his tattoos dance. One of a snake, and one of a pirate. I tear my eyes away from his muscles and try not to imagine the story behind each tattoo.

He works here. Somehow that's even worse. Like I've graduated from stalking Shawn Next to stalking his neighbour.

As I look away I notice a signed Shawn Next poster on the wall and cringe. I have to get out of here; my tolerance for humiliation is at capacity. The boy disappears into the kitchen. This is my chance. I shove what's left of the cherry pie in my mouth because I'm not sure when I'll be eating again. I squeeze out of the booth, grab my suitcase and stalk to the chrome bar, ready to duck sideways if the boy emerges again. I ask the waitress behind the bar for the bill and it takes three tries till I realize I'm supposed to say *Check please*. She nods and scurries off. As I turn sideways I catch the two baseball-cap-clad men watching me.

'How about I buy you a drink, sweetheart?' says the one closest. He seems amused by me. His dull eyes travel up and down my body.

His cheeks are red with veiny splotches that make it look like pink ink is spreading across his pale skin. He's wearing a chequered shirt with shiny snap buttons that barely covers his gut. A sliver of pink escapes it.

'No, thank you,' I say.

'Come on, just one.' He makes his voice softer, as if I could be lulled.

'No, thank you,' I say again, injecting a little more ice into it this time.

'Leave it, she's not even hot,' the man mumbles to his friend. The friend, who looks like a miniature weasel, snorts and keeps drinking.

I whirl. 'Huh?'

'What's wrong? Don't understand English?' the larger one snaps.

'I'm ... I'm from London,' I say as if that changes something. 'Of course I understand English.'

'Well fuck off back to London,' says the smaller one. They both laugh.

It feels like this is all happening very slowly. Like I'm weaving through treacle.

I spot the boy. Even from the corner of my eye I recognize him from the way he holds himself, his broad shoulders and confident gait. He's come back from the kitchen and I was too busy dealing with these losers to notice. I look away and keep my chin up, but in my peripheral I can sense him standing there, my skin prickling at having him so close.

He's probably pleased more people are telling me off.

'Did you hear my buddy, go back where you came from, ugly bitch,' says the man's weaselly friend. They both laugh deeply, as if they've reached the peak of comedic genius.

The boy rounds the counter. He is holding one of those square buckets full of dirty dishes.

'It's not for you to decide where I go,' I say. My voice is small.

Nice one, Nadia, call the Guinness Book of World Records *because you have just set one for the lamest comeback ever.*

'If you're bent on staying maybe you can make yourself useful,' says the pink-faced man. He makes a lewd gesture.

It's nothing I haven't heard before. I've been catcalled from cars and outside pubs just like any teenage girl.

But I've never heard it when I'm all alone in a strange place. From a man who is big, and who a minute prior looked at me hungrily. A man who is now looking at me like he doesn't even need permission to take what he wants. It makes me nauseous and my cheeks flare up in shame. I stagger backwards, stumbling into the boy, who sets his bucket of grimy dishes down with a clatter.

Is he going to shout at me again?

He walks over and plants himself between me and the vile men, his large frame casting a shadow over me.

'Apologize to the lady,' he says, surprising me. But he says it in the way where it suggests he knows that's not

89

going to happen. The suggestion is just a precursor. The larger man frowns, his red face creasing up and turning him into more of a pig.

'Go back to your dishes, busboy,' he says, waving his hand in dismissal.

'Earn those dollars while you can. Till we put that wall up,' his smaller friend echoes.

Again, they laugh. I'm horrified. The boy stands his ground, stepping closer to me until his fingers are inches from mine. I swallow. He smells way too good for a guy working in a sweaty kitchen.

I decide to say something random. The way Lizzy would.

'Yeah? Well you look like a pig in a shirt,' I tell him. Anger flashes across his face. 'Yeah that's right, you heard me. And your friend here looks like a manky bug-eyed weasel.'

He lunges at me, like he's going to grab me by the collar, but the boy is quicker.

He lands a punch across the larger one's jaw, and it's like his knuckles slapped against a pancake. The large pig man punches the boy in the gut, and the sheer force of it sends him crashing into a nearby table. He punches back, but the weasel man jumps in, knocking him to his knees.

The larger one is nursing his cheek, his jaw raised and red, shouting racist obscenities at us both. Weasel man punches the boy in the stomach a second time, making him double over with a grunt. And I'm just standing there, watching it all unfold, witnessing a boy getting beaten up all because of me.

The smaller man goes to kick him, and everything goes into slow motion. Something echoes in my mind.

Number 12 – Stand up for yourself

Number 12 – Stand up for yourself

Number 12 – Stand the fuck up for yourself!

Lizzy's voice is so loud in my head that for a second, I think she is behind me. And when she inevitably isn't, the words melt into red-hot anger. I know Lizzy meant stand up to my family but I also know she wrote it because she thought I was a coward. I don't want to be a coward. I lurch forward.

I'm not sure what I'm doing but suddenly I've grabbed the bucket of dishes and crashed it down on the head of the little weaselly man. And then my nails are on his face. I land a deep scratch and he howls. His friend pulls me off but I turn and my knee finds his crotch through his Walmart mom jeans. He crumbles to the floor. I kick out.

'You're done, Fran, get the hell out of here,' I hear someone yell from the bar. I kick out again and again.

I'm not aware that we've won the battle till the boy pulls me off the pink-faced guy, and I'm still screaming and cursing in Russian as the boy drags me backwards out of the diner. He somehow remembers my suitcase.

'Calm down, it's okay, it's done,' says the boy. He releases me and I flail in place for a second like a bird learning to fly. Then I realize we are out of the diner, outside by the kerb, and his strong hand is on my arm. He's waiting for me to settle down, to get my breath back, and to stop shaking with anger.

He's leading me to a red car, his hand hot and heavy against my clammy skin. The car is old and shiny and pretty, like something from an old movie. He ushers me into it, puts my suitcase in the back, and I take the passenger seat while he starts the engine.

Who is this guy, swooping in and sweeping us away like a getaway driver?

We drive in silence as I catch my breath and try and figure out what the hell just happened.

We pull into a gas station and the boy turns to me, his dark eyes flooded with concern. He looks totally different when he's not full of rage.

'You okay?' he asks.

'I'm fine. You?'

As the raw adrenaline fizzles into weariness, I'm slowly starting to realize I'm in a car with a boy I don't know. I don't know where I am either, but somehow, I know I'm safer here than in that diner.

'I'm sorry about what they said, about the wall,' I say.

'I'm used to it.' He shrugs. Gaze drifting to the neon of the station.

'I've never heard people say that kind of thing.'

'Well you aren't Latina,' he says a little awkwardly.

I shrug. 'No, I mean we don't have a wall.'

He nods. '*And* you're a pretty white girl, you're probably not used to niche insults getting hurled at you.'

He thinks I'm pretty. But the way he says it sounds more like an insult than a compliment.

'True. But I'm also Russian. All we get is Bond villains, and a category on Pornhub. So, I get my share of hate but it's not usually *that* intense.'

Shut up, Nadia, why are you rambling utter nonsense?

He chuckles, and it makes his sharp jawline flex. 'How do you know it's a category on Pornhub?'

Oh God, now we're talking about sex. My stomach is churning on overdrive.

93

Boys at school told me. I shrug my shoulders. He laughs. I don't.

He rubs his jaw. It's starting to turn blue.

'Your face looks sore,' I say, reaching out to touch it and pulling back.

'I've never punched anyone before, it fucking hurts.'

'*You've* never punched anyone?' My eyes widen.

'Just 'cause I'm Mexican and have tattoos does not mean I go around punching people.'

He cocks a fluffy brow. I'm quiet. I did make my assumptions, he's right about that. I feel myself flush. This conversation isn't going my way.

'Nice car,' I say. I don't know anything about cars but it's old and shiny and so desperately clean it looks like he puts a lot of man-hours into cleaning it with microfibre cloths.

'Thanks, it's a '63 Cadillac.' His voice is thick with pride, as if I had asked him about his kid.

'Cool,' I nod because I have nothing else to say. Is a '63 better than '64, is it slightly worse than a '62? Or is it the other way around? I open and close my mouth a few times.

'Thanks for standing up for me,' I say. Somehow the *thank you* sticks a little in my throat.

'You didn't seem to need the help. That guy looked like he had been attacked by a cheetah.'

I flex my fingers, which are starting to ache, my nails stinging at the nail beds. I can't believe I clawed at his face.

There's a long awkward silence as we both catch our breath and stare out at the gas station.

'I got you fired,' I say quietly. I just spread misery everywhere I go.

'It's fine. My boss was a jerk. Buy me a Slurpee and we are even,' he says. His tone is friendly.

I shift in the leather of my seat and nod, though I'm not sure what a Slurpee is.

I follow him into the convenience store, and he fetches two large plastic cups. He points at the colourful row of churning flavoured ice.

'What flavour do you want?' he asks.

I gawk at the giant machine. A far cry from our off-brand one-flavour red in Windsor. So, Slurpees are Slush Puppies then, I realize. 'I'm not sure, what do you recommend?'

'How about Dr Pepper? It's the only flavour worth a damn.'

I nod. I feel like an idiot; can't I even pick a Slurpee

flavour or say anything interesting? Maybe I only have the emotional capacity to sob, eat or punch things.

I swipe my card by the till, grateful Lizzy and I got our own cards last year and that my mum won't see my middle-of-nowhere purchase in St. Louis. Lizzy and I were going to work and save up for Ibiza. In the end I'm just left here with the money I earned via babysitting and helping Dad. I haven't even touched it until now. Each pound spent meant Lizzy and I were no longer going to Spain.

I think Lizzy would be fine with my dipping into my Ibiza savings to buy a guy a Slush Puppy for punching someone in the face for my honour.

I follow him out of the store. He sits down on the kerb and hands me the icy drink.

I gulp. He gulps too. The sound of slurping fills the space between us.

'We call them Slush Puppies,' I tell him. 'Which I guess makes a lot less sense.'

'Slush Puppies,' he repeats, examining his drink.

The frozen Dr Pepper tastes amazing. I drink too much at once and squint at the resulting brain freeze.

'My name is Nadia,' I offer after a beat.

'Nah-di-aa,' he pronounces as if he's learning the word. 'My name is Francisco.' *Slurp. Slurp. Slurp.*

'Like San Francisco?'

He winces. 'Nope.'

I wait for an explanation but he doesn't give me one. I suddenly remember how he yelled at me.

'Can I call you Fran?'

His voice is hard. '*No.*'

'Do people call you Franny?'

'If people called me Franny I would drive off a cliff.'

'You would never drive off a cliff,' I say.

His eyes narrow. A coldness sweeps over them.

'And why not? Think you know me?' His hostility is back. I tilt my chin towards the car.

'You would never drive off a cliff, because you drive a '63 Cadillac.'

He grins a little through his scowl. Even though I think he decided at some point that he'll never smile again.

Just like I did.

His Slurpee hits the end sound. He shakes it, trying to loosen the icy bits at the bottom. 'So, do you need me to drive you somewhere?'

'I have a flight tomorrow,' I lie, even though that isn't really an answer to his question.

'Oh, should I drive you to your hotel?'

'No, it's okay. I'll walk or take the train.'

His eyes narrow again. 'What train?'

I fumble with my Slurpee straw. 'The train to the airport.'

His gaze is intent on me for a while.

'There is no train to the airport from here.'

'Oh,' I fumble. 'I'll take a taxi then.'

'You sure? That's an expensive trip.'

I nod my head. I need him gone. I need to regroup. To think about what I can do. To craft that text I'm terrified of writing. To switch on my phone and see Larissa's reply.

Larissa will probably have to tell my parents that I skipped my flight; they would expect to talk to me by evening.

'It was nice to meet you.' Fran tips his Slurpee at me. I look at his red knuckles.

'That's a lie but thanks, nice to meet you too,' I say.

'That makes two lies.' He nods and makes his way to the car. 'Good luck.'

I watch him drive off. I pull out my phone and curse at the low battery. This is it, the moment I have to admit defeat. Maybe it's for the best. I type in the message. If Larissa has already told my parents then I don't know how I'll ever explain this to them. It's madness and they can't understand my madness because they can't understand my pain. I turn my phone on and see sixteen missed calls from Larissa and one text from Dad.

> Mama wants to know when you're back from Larissa's?

So, she hasn't told them yet?

Ignoring the messages that start to flood in I begin to type mine to Larissa.

> Hi Larissa, I'm sorry if the previous text worried you. I had a plan to try and meet Shawn Next after the concert, but it didn't work. I'm in St. Louis (where he's from) and I'm safe. I will use my savings and try to be back at yours tomorrow night. I know even 1000 apologies won't cut it. But I'll explain when I get back. Please don't hate me. I'm sorry.

I prepare to send this and plan to switch my phone immediately into airplane mode again. My anxiety over her missed calls has already curdled the cold Slurpee in my belly but I'm too much of a coward right now to call her back or to read the rest of her messages.

Suddenly, I see a flash of red and then Francisco is pulling back into the car park. He gets out of his cherry-hued car and stares down at me. He has broad shoulders, and a calm intensity that instantly makes me feel silly as I stare back, straw pinched between my teeth.

"What?' I say. My tone is even less friendly than I intended. He looks like he's second-guessing himself.

'I think you might need a place to stay. You can sleep at my house, if you need it.'

'Is that your pitch?'

'Oh no, I have a full PowerPoint presentation ready. The first ten pages are about my hypothesis that you have no hotel room reserved and not a lot of money on you, and the later part is about how you are sitting in a parking lot looking sad and crying in a city you are not familiar with. It then leads into my conclusion that I should offer you my couch and my Wi-Fi because I'm a decent human being.'

'How do I know you're not crazy?'

'I'm the one who caught you trying to get in a celebrity's house, remember?'

'I knocked,' I say.

'Look it's no hair off my back, I thought I would be nice and offer.'

'The expression is *no skin off my back*, not *hair*.'

Fran nearly smiles. 'How about the expression *beggars can't be choosers*?'

'I don't need any help.' I know I sound grumpy and petulant but I can't help it. I hate being pitied.

Then I realize something. If I go to his house I can save money and I can see if Shawn Next's parents come home in the end, then I can still ask them about the pyjamas. And I'll have enough money for a flight in the morning, which I can book from his house.

I get up and he helps me load my suitcase in the car.

'So, you travelled all the way from . . . ?'

'England.'

'All the way from England to see Shawn Next? In St. Louis, when he moved out of his parents' house years ago?' Weirdly, he sounds a little bitter.

My stomach somersaults. He still called it his parents' house. 'You seem to know a lot about Shawn Next for someone who doesn't like him.'

'I never said I didn't like him.'

I promise myself I won't gawk at Sean's house when we arrive, I will act completely uninterested.

Fran drives slowly and in silence till we reach his house.

I have never slept in a boy's house. I have never even been in a boy's house before. Not unless they were related to me. Fran's house is odd; it looks like it was wealthy once but has been left for a long time. A sort of dilapidated niceness – unkept, abandoned. My house is far from luxurious – it's a small three-bedroom in Slough crammed with my two brothers and my parents and myself – but it's very lived-in. There's always the smell of food, and light, and the sound of voices. But this house is cold and still. Where is everyone?

I don't ask what time his parents will be home because something holds me back. Something about that question seems wrong.

'There isn't much in the fridge,' he tells me. 'Unless you're fond of old apples.'

'I exclusively eat old apples,' I say. *You sound deranged, Nadia. Stop trying to be witty and say something normal!*

'Your house smells nice.' *No, it doesn't.*

Fran gives me an odd look as if he knows that his house doesn't exactly smell of roses. It smells of old things, yard sale trinkets that should have been dusted and thrown away but have been left as food for the moths. It smells a little like my grandma Viera's closet.

His house is so quiet.

'I'll make ramen,' he says decidedly.

Fran makes us two packets of ramen, and for something whose flavour comes in a shiny square packet it's actually pretty delicious. My mum would call it astronaut food, but it's very tasty and he's gone to the trouble of upgrading it with his own touches, covering the ramen in spring onions and adding a runny egg.

Besides, travelling has made me hungry, and since I've got to America, I've been craving food at all times.

'It's delicious,' I say, gulping it down.

'Gets you through. I'm not a great cook. But I can do the simple things.'

I feel a little guilty suddenly and wonder how often Fran eats ramen.

My gaze wanders to the kitchen. It's a mess but doesn't look like it's been cooked in – piles of dirty dishes by the sink but no pots and pans. The open-face cupboards are stocked with a few tins and packets but that's it. Suddenly

I realize maybe the diner let him have free food. Maybe I've cost him his income *and* his food source.

I excuse myself and ask for the bathroom. On my way back, I take my time and observe a wall full of portraits. There aren't any recent ones of Fran but there are a lot of him from his childhood, smiling toothily next to a woman and man who are very clearly his parents. His dad looks like him, but his eyes are more serious, and he wears an army uniform in a lot of the shots. His mum has long dark hair and beautiful brown eyes. The three of them look happy.

Where are his parents?

I spot a photo that makes me catch my breath.

He's young in it, but it's unmissable. There's a photo of a ten-or-so-year-old Fran, his hand slung around the shoulder of a ten-year-old Shawn Next. I squeal and skip into the living room holding the frame triumphantly.

'You know Shawn Next,' I announce.

Fran looks taken aback. Then his eyes narrow at what's in my hands.

'My mom liked that picture,' he says as a way of explanation. His tone is glacial.

I sit across from him and I can't help but grin a little. 'How did you meet? What's he like? How well did you know him?'

'There it is.' Fran points his finger at me. 'That exact expression. As if my whole existence is defined by my knowing Shawn Next.' He sounds angry and my smile leaves. *What did I say?*

'He's just a person,' says Fran.

He's not just a person, he's a god, I think to myself. But mercifully I keep my mouth shut.

Fran gets up. Scrapes the rest of his plate out into the bin and leaves the room. He comes back with a blanket for me, a sheet and a pillow. He dumps them on the couch. He doesn't bother making my bed. Then he leaves.

Even though it seems weird to sleep at someone's house when they are angry with you, I'm too tired to figure anything else out. I pull the rough blanket over my eyes and drift.

CHAPTER 6

Honey and frothed milk

Grief is like a weird type of alarm clock. Every day when I wake up my first thought is *Lizzy is dead*. She doesn't exist in this reality. She is not alive in this world. As counter-intuitive as it might seem, I think part of me keeps hoping that I'm going to wake up one day and it will have actually all been a bad dream. That seems less likely every morning that I put more space between the before and the after.

That's another weird thing. Grief starts to be your measuring cup for time. It's not just a Wednesday, it's the *39th day since Lizzy died Wednesday*. And it's not just Bonfire Night, it's the first Bonfire Night I will spend without Lizzy. Without watching fireworks on the bridge with her. And this isn't just a Monday morning in St. Louis, it's a Monday morning in which I'm reminded that Lizzy is still dead.

That's my first thought when I wake up. *Lizzy is gone.*

My next thought is *Why the hell is Fran looming over me?* I'm screaming, arms thrashing about, legs kicking out. He reaches out for me but I'm skittering along the couch away from him, my hands thrown up in front of me for protection because he's a boy and it's dark and I'm scared. He backs away and raises his hands in the air like he's surrendering to me.

'I'm not going to hurt you, Nadia,' he says gently. 'You were having a nightmare. I heard you and came down.'

'I was.' It's not a question. I know I was – it's just something to say. My cheeks are hot and my breath hasn't slowed yet.

'Are you okay?'

'No,' I say finally. 'I'm not.'

Fran doesn't prod, he just silently leaves the room and returns with a glass of hot frothy milk with honey and cinnamon. It's a weird concoction but it's soothing.

'My mom used to make it,' he explains, nodding at the

drink. A few loose curls fall in his eyes, and I clench my fists to stop myself from sweeping them off his face.

I don't ask where his mum is. I know there is a reason for the stillness of his house. There's a reason his mother used to make his milk and now she doesn't any more. There is a reason I used to sleep calmly through the night. Telling people your reasons doesn't make them go away.

'Who is Lizzy?' he asks when I've drained my glass. I can feel a milk moustache turn my lip sticky. I must have said her name in my sleep. No one has pointed that out before. No one has come to wake me from my nightmares before.

'She was my best friend.' I think Fran can sense that Lizzy *was* my best friend in the same way that his mother *used* to make frothy milk. So, he doesn't ask. I volunteer the information myself.

'She left me this list of things I was supposed to do to get over her death. Getting our pyjamas signed by Shawn Next was the biggest thing on the list.'

'Oh.' His *oh* is jam-packed with meaning. 'Like a death list?'

'Sure, you can call it that. She called it *healing girl summer*. Like a hot girl summer, but you know, *healing*.'

My chest heaves up and down and I try to ease into that

rhythm. To stop any potential panic attack in its tracks. *Not sure about how healing this journey has been so far.*

'Have you finished the rest of the list?'

I thumb the coarse blanket. 'Not really.'

'I'm going to get some cookies for us,' he says, fetching a paper pack that says *Pepperidge Farm* on it. He lays the pack between us on the couch, angling it towards me. I think the cookies are his way of asking me to tell him more, so I do.

I tell Fran about Larissa, the ticket to New York and the robbery. I don't tell him about how Lizzy died. I haven't been able to talk about it without a lump forming in my throat. Not yet.

'How many things are on this list of yours?'

'Sixteen.'

'How many have you done?'

'Three, if I count punching those guys at the diner as standing up for myself.'

'Oh,' he says again.

'There are some easy ones, like *Dye your hair a wild colour.*'

'And did you do that one?'

'No.'

But he doesn't say anything beyond that. I kind of wish

he would. Dyeing my hair a wild colour is probably one of the easiest things on the list, but I didn't want to deal with my mother's disappointment. Didn't want to deal with hearing her thoughts again about the list. Didn't want to deal with the hatred I would feel for her when she inevitably criticized or dismissed it. But it's irrelevant now. I had one chance to make a dent in the list and I blew it. Now I'm alone in Missouri on a stranger's crouch.

'Get some sleep,' Fran tells me. His expression is a little softer than before. He doesn't look at me as he switches the light off.

When my fatigue outweighs my fear of another nightmare, I drift off again.

Somehow, I wish Lizzy had written *Sleep over at a boy's house* on her list, so I would have another thing I could cross off.

But I think she thought that was beyond my capabilities.

Later in the morning Fran makes me coffee. It all feels very grown up and I resist my deepest urge to comment on it and make an arse of myself again. Instead I act like boys have made me coffee before, and I lie and say I take it black like him, which makes me cough and gag. Fran is also cooking breakfast. He doesn't know it but, in my head, he is cemented as *Fran*. I can smell eggs and bacon and . . . something else. His right bicep flexes as he flips the omelette over with a diner level of expertise. Then he blows a curly lock of a hair out of his eyesight and catches me staring.

'What?'

'What is that?' I point at an unravelled cylindrical cardboard container with a bit of dough peeking out.

'Pillsbury Doughboy biscuits,' he says, as if it's the most obvious thing in the world.

'What's a Pillsbury Doughboy?'

'This little guy.' He points at an adorable white cartoon character on the side of the packaging. Then he pops the biscuits in the oven.

Fran sets out two plates, and I get the vague feeling that he has done this before.

'Do you go to school?' I ask. 'Or college?'

'No, I dropped out of high school and got my GED.'

'Oh cool,' I say stupidly. I have no idea what a GED is. 'How come?'

'More hours to work. Plus, I failed my SATs, which meant no direct access to a good four-year school so I might as well transfer after two years, you know?'

I nod as if I know but I still have no idea what he's

talking about. We have a completely different system in the UK. Fran seems to notice.

'My high school was no good, no electives, bad teachers, crappy sports teams, it would be hard to get noticed by a good college anyway, and even then, they are like thirty thousand bucks a year. I take a few community college classes though; I almost have enough credits to transfer.' He pauses briefly, as if lost in thought. 'Did you sleep all right?'

'I did, the couch is comfy, thanks.'

I start to think about what kind of girls Fran might have had over. Does he have a girlfriend? How old is he? He looks about my age. Maybe a year older.

'How old are you?' I ask rounding the island, which like everything else in the house is a little run-down.

'Do I look under age?' he asks. I frown. I'm pretty sure I've had an indignant crease in-between my eyebrows since I met him. Though he hasn't been a ball of sunshine either.

'I'm nearly nineteen,' he says seriously.

'I'm nearly eighteen,' I say. (I'm precisely nine months away from being eighteen.)

'Where are your parents?' I ask as he slips the egg from the pan on to my plate.

'They are abroad,' he says. I can tell he is lying but I don't press him.

My gaze drifts and lands on the shutters of the house next door. I haven't spotted any movement out there. There weren't any lights on last night. Would it be psychotic to try and knock on the door again? I know he said Shawn doesn't live here any more, but surely his parents could help me. He never said they didn't still live here, and clearly they do if he got so mad when he saw me there.

I look at my phone, still on airplane mode. Charging idly on the island. I *have* to switch it on. Larissa will be worried sick. And I have to book a flight.

I look out at the house again through the window longingly. Fran has trusted me and let me into his house. It would kind of be an insult to try again.

'You know,' he says carefully, 'none of them live there any more. The whole family moved.'

He sounds a little sad when he says this. I swallow and turn to him.

I can't believe I just assumed they live there because of Shawn's biography and Fran's reaction. Shawn's a kazillionaire, why would his parents still live in the same house he grew up in?

113

God I'm so stupid.

'So, you let me be embarrassed? Humiliated? Even though you knew they don't even live there?'

I've stood up, and I'm surprised to find that I'm quite angry. Fran just let me think he had caught me spying on them. He got so angry. For no reason.

'It's just . . .' He hesitates. 'You weren't the first. There have been . . . *others*, like you.'

He says the last bit ominously. Did he . . . Did he think I was dangerous or something? What does he mean *others like me*?

'So, what, you thought I was just another dodgy, desperate, wide-eyed fan?'

'I didn't know your story, Nadia.' He is looking straight at me, dark eyes boring into me.

The fact that he now pities me just makes it all worse.

'You gave me that whole lecture about privacy when they don't even live there!'

'In all fairness, the people in that house *do* deserve privacy.'

'Unbelievable!' I gawk at him. We are both silent for a beat.

Tears fall freely down my face, I can't stop them. He looks a little remorseful.

I want to stop crying but I can't fight the grief.

'Look, I've been thinking,' he ventures carefully. 'I do have *an* address . . . In LA, for Shawn I mean. I could give it to you. But you have to use it responsibly.'

I look up through my wet lashes, surprised.

'So, I shouldn't break in and lie naked in his bed in waiting?'

Fran's eyes widen as if I'm serious.

'I'm kidding! Thanks, that's very kind of you. Honestly. But I'm running out of money and I'm already in so much trouble. I don't think I can fly out to LA. I won't be able to afford the ticket back to England.'

Fran seems to stare at some point on the wall. He rolls back on to his heels.

'We could,' he starts, 'we could drive there. I mean, I could drive you.'

'Why would you do that?'

'Well I don't have a job any more, I have a little money saved up, from working, and my dad sends me money *sooo* . . .' He scratches the back of his head. 'I could pay for gas, and I haven't taken any time off in about two years. I've always wanted to drive down Route 66. I've been when I was little, but not since fixing up the Cadillac.'

'Route 66?'

'It's a famous scenic highway full of Americana, weird stuff like the biggest cowboy hat in the world.'

I don't really know what to say.

'I've never been to California,' Fran adds. I know there are other reasons that have nothing to do with the ones he has just listed.

If you keep moving then you won't have to stop and feel the stillness. The absence of sounds that were once there. Lizzy's laugh. The clink of a spoon hitting the edges of a cup as it stirs honey into frothed milk.

He wants to escape, just like me.

I smile and say, 'Me neither.'

CHAPTER 7

Like Thelma and Louise?

From the start of the trip, a part of me knew that meeting Shawn was a long shot. Even now, with a proper address, a million things could go wrong. But I stopped caring about odds a long time ago. Because I also know that once upon a time Lizzy had all the odds in her favour. Odds mean nothing.

Why do I know this? Because when someone you love is sick, Google is your only bedfellow. In the dark hours of the night you google the crap out of everything. *Is my best friend going to die? What should you say when someone finds out they have cancer? What do you wear to a funeral?*

The answers will scare you and Google will tell you other shit that will comfort you. Like that Lizzy was one of only five thousand teens a year who developed cancer, that with proper healthcare, which we have, she was very likely to survive.

But Google doesn't know the future, it just knows statistics.

Sometimes, I wish my parents had thought to just take my damn phone away. Because one day I googled what death looked like and I realized, point-blank, that Lizzy was dying. Did you know that death is an actual process? You can see it. Feel it coming. You can smell it. I thought one day someone just doesn't wake up. I did not know that you can see death coming and pulling that person away from you. Shadowy black fingers reaching down and trying to pluck them away.

Sometimes someone is dying for days and you can see it happening. But you can't stop it. It's in their restless hands. It's in the slow breathing that stops sometimes all together and you hold your own breath waiting, hoping it will resume. It's in the lack of interest in things they once loved – like the time I played a Shawn Next song for Lizzy and her head didn't move, it was like she couldn't hear it. She was done with Shawn Next. She was done with the living.

It's this restlessness that is the most terrifying thing of all. Sometimes Lizzy looked like she was at a train station, checking for her ticket, scanning the timetable, shuffling her hands nervously. She looked like she had somewhere to be. And it broke my heart, because that *somewhere* was a place I could not follow.

The worst question I've ever been asked in my life is whether I would like to help pick out what she would wear to the grave. To help pick the colours they would paint her with. 'You know so much about make-up,' her mother Natalia said, that half-dreaming denial on her face. *What's Lizzy's favourite lipstick?* They asked me kindly. As if they were doing me a favour by letting me pick.

A paralyzing shudder creeps up my skin.

I'll never get over this. I'll just feel this way for the rest of my life.

My brain walk ends and I'm back in Fran's kitchen.

'Jeez, why are you crying again?' says Fran. But he doesn't say it in a mean way. More in a *there is a girl crying at my kitchen island and I don't know what to do* type of way.

'Taking me to California. It's a nice offer,' I sob.

119

He rounds the island and hands me a tissue as if it's something he's seen people do on TV.

'If it's a nice offer then take it. You got something else you need to be doing?'

'Not really,' I sob again. 'I'm suspended from school.'

His eyes go round. 'What for?'

'Dragging a girl down the hallway by her hair.'

'*Dios mio*,' says Fran. I can tell he is suppressing a laugh. He scratches at his curly hair. 'You've got a violent streak, Nadia. Maybe I shouldn't be offering to drive you across the country.'

I know he's joking but I sob harder. There's a black pit inside of me and it's expanding.

'Hey, hey, hey,' Fran says a little awkwardly, like he is trying to calm a frenzied horse. 'I'm kidding. Look, you're suspended. I'm fired. We are a couple of outlaws, let's go drive across country. Screw it.'

I sniffle. 'Like Thelma and Louise?'

Fran cringes. 'Sure. Like Thelma and Louise.'

I know it cost him a lot to give me that one.

I pack my stuff, which takes the whole of one minute. Fran disappears and comes back with a backpack. He packs snacks, a few bottles of water, blankets, pillows and a flashlight.

I take five deep breaths and switch the airplane mode off on my phone. Then sign into Fran's Wi-Fi.

The slew of incoming texts is instant. I push away the thought of roaming charges and read.

I scan the first few friendly ones from Larissa that pre-date Vanya picking me up.

How was the concert?

Send me photos!

Hope you got the autographs, how exciting! Don't miss your flight!

I cringe at this. Hot shame swirls like lava in my belly.

Where the hell are you Nadia?

I'm really worried I've called 60 times. Answer me?

What do you mean you're not done with the list? Nadia explain yourself?

Nadia please. Where are you?

YOU WANT ME NOT TO WORRY????

There are many more messages in that same vein. And one video from my brother Stepa, a TikTok compilation of sibling pranks.

It's late Monday morning here, late afternoon in the UK. There's a notification from Dad and my finger hovers over it. I feel like I'm about to puke.

Larissa told me, it reads. *I haven't told your mum because I don't want to give her a heart attack. You need to be back by Monday.*

So, Larissa went to my dad instead of her sister. She probably didn't want to deal with Mum's screaming. It makes me feel a little bit better that she doesn't yet know. But I've run out of time.

There's a brief text from Mum asking about the living room remote malfunctioning.

I answer Mum, giving her detailed instructions on how to use the remote and a few lies about my homework.

Then, squinting from the anxiety, I text Larissa back.

Larissa, it's a long story but I'm following Shawn Next to get the autographs. A chance to meet him has come up . . . and I have to take it. I'm going to be gone for a few more days. I'm really sorry. Please don't tell Mama anything. If there is any way you and Dad can stall I will owe you FOR LIFE. I'm safe. I'm fine. I'm in zero danger. I will be back soon. I'm begging you. It's like you said . . . I need this.

The last phrase, using her own claim against her, is a little manipulative but hopefully it buys me a couple of days.

I add another text that says *Yellow blue bus.*

It's our inside joke. Grandma told us that's how they would teach visiting Americans to tell Russian girls they loved them in the Soviet Union. Because *Ya lublu vas* (I love you) sounds like *yellow blue bus.*

I send it off and squeal nervously when it registers as delivered.

Immediately it shows Larissa typing back. I turn

the phone back to airplane mode. I can't deal with this right now.

I spent the last eight months trying to disassociate from my pain.

Sometimes too well: missing my stops on the tube, forgetting my keys in random places, coming to the end of an exam and realizing I only filled a third of it in ... I push away the thought of my family, of Larissa, of my phone.

I *have* to do this. Lizzy's voice is loud in my head, spurring me on. Take the leap. *Jump, Nadia.* And I do.

By the time we get into Fran's cherry-red car and he drives us out of the suburbs, across the city, through the state, and up towards Route 66, I've forgotten all about it.

CHAPTER 8

Dr Pepper was a pharmacist from Texas

We are in the car headed 'west' as Fran calls it.

'Usually people take the interstate,' he tells me. 'But this is the far more scenic route. Even though we have to drive up a few hours till we reach it.'

It takes half a day until we are technically on Route 66. Though Fran isn't showing any signs of being tired.

I try to stop myself from staring at his tattoos as he points at things. I noticed the snake and the pirate yesterday but now I see the name Sofia in calligraphy. A girlfriend perhaps? There's also a skull, some flowers and ...

'Is that a Teletubby?' I say in shock.

'It's Po. He was my favourite when I was little.'

I can't believe this brooding, sombre boy has a Teletubby tattoo on his arm.

'Well I like the snake and the pirate,' I say casually. 'But what's this one?'

I point at the cursive name but misjudge the distance and accidentally brush my finger against it.

Fran cracks a half smile.

'The *pirate* as you called him is Captain Crunch, you know from the cereal. The name . . .' He stalls for a moment. 'That's my mom's name.'

I nod but don't push the topic further. Instead I grill him on his love of cartoons and cereal.

We stop briefly at a dilapidated Chinese restaurant from the fifties to get gas at the old petrol station next to it. I gaze out of my open window. Everything around here has that sunburnt look to it.

Fran points out old neon signs to me and explains what breeze block porches are (cement blocks with holes in them to let the breeze in, not very fascinating) and why Route 66 businesses are slowly all dying out and being replaced by corporate wannabes. I snap pictures and put them in a hidden folder on my old phone.

'Have you ever driven down any part of Route 66?' I ask him.

'Yeah but only when I was little, my dad said he would take me again someday, after we fixed the Cadillac. But we never went.'

I want to ask why they never ended up going, and where his parents actually are, and whether he fixed up the Cadillac himself or with his father, but I don't. I've invaded Fran's privacy enough by staying in his home, and going to his place of work. I'll wait till he feels like telling me more.

During the drive Fran tells me nature facts and lectures me about the old cars that are used as decorations for businesses along the route.

He tells me their history and make.

I giggle a bit about the fact that Fran seems to be a seventy-year-old man trapped in a teenager's body.

We take a small break by an outdoor crystal shop that doesn't have an attendant and works by the honour system instead. I pick up a little pink crystal for Larissa, and a beautiful purple stone for each of my brothers.

I don't know how I will give the stones to them since they don't know I've gone down Route 66.

'What else is on that list of yours?' Fran asks as a sign tells us we are nearing the state border.

'It's not my list, it's Lizzy's list.' I don't know why my voice comes out as defensive on that. I guess because I see Lizzy's list and my failure to complete it as a burden. And I don't want him to think it's *my* list.

'All right,' he says temperately. 'What's on Lizzy's list then?'

I sigh and pull out the piece of paper, the folds made soft by the number of times I've opened it. I know it by heart but Fran doesn't need to know that.

'I've done three things on it as I said,' I explain. 'I asked Joey out, stood up for myself.'

'Asked Joey out, huh? Is he handsome?'

'Not really.' I'm not sure why I just lied. Joey has baby-blue eyes and a rugby six pack. If you open a dictionary to the word *handsome*, Joey's portrait would be right there. But I felt like lying about it. Maybe because he rejected me.

'What else?'

I consult the list. 'I've *Screamed into the void*, though I sort of butchered that, then there's *Eat sweets for dinner, Play bingo with old ladies, Open mic night, Do something that scares you*. I think she wanted me to read my poetry in public, which I've never done . . .' I forget what I was saying for a minute as we pass a sign that reads LARGEST WOMBAT STATUE IN THE WORLD, NEXT RIGHT. 'And *Go viral on social media for doing something cool, Have a Gosling kiss—*'

Fran interrupts me.

'What's a Gosling kiss?'

'Like in *The Notebook*,' I tell him.

His expression is blank. I'm guessing he hasn't seen *The Notebook*. He probably sticks to black-and-white footage of people talking about cars.

'Like Ryan Gosling? It's the kiss at the end of a romantic film. The one where the guy grabs the girl and a song usually plays and it's all epic and grand. That's a movie kiss. A Gosling kiss.'

'I see,' says Fran but I'm pretty sure he has no clue what I'm talking about. 'You write poetry?'

I shrink back into the red leather. 'Not really.'

'She wouldn't have put the open mic thing on the list if you didn't write poetry.'

You didn't know her, I want to snap. But he's right,

Lizzy is the only one who ever read my poems. And she liked them.

'Yeah, you're right.' I shrug. 'She always wanted me to read my poems out loud, preferably at some artsy event in London, where a hot young writer would hear me and fall immediately in love. But that's never happening.'

'The reading your poetry out loud thing, or the falling in love?'

I blush. 'Both.'

Fran frowns. 'Okay, what scares you?'

I realize Fran is back to talking about the list.

Do something that scares you.

A hell of a lot scares me. I'm afraid my brothers will die. I'm afraid I will spend the rest of my life with fear and despair and anxiety churning in the place behind my belly button. I'm afraid I'll never amount to anything. But none of these fears are things that you can *do*. Lizzy probably meant something ballsy, like rock climbing or skydiving.

'I'm scared of ghosts,' I tell him.

Not the ones that haunt the halls of manors, but the ones that haunt the corners of your brain. I don't tell him that . . .

He nods, as if he knows exactly what I mean, and we spend the next half-hour's drive in silence.

'Aside from the Shawn Next challenge,' Fran ventures, 'it doesn't really seem to be a hard list.'

That sounds like a criticism.

'*Scream into the void, Go skinny-dipping,* this isn't exactly Shakespeare. Just teen girl stuff,' I say defensively. I hate myself for being dismissive of Lizzy's list but I don't like the way he insinuates that I could have finished it but chose not to. 'Hot girl summer stuff.'

'Err, yeah, what *is* hot girl summer?' Fran asks.

'Fun bucket-list items you do in the summer. We were going to do them together, but she ran out of time and rewrote the list just for me.' My voice goes funny and tight at the end. Fran doesn't say anything for a minute.

'Eating candy for dinner sounds easy enough,' he says.

When I don't answer him, he continues, 'What did she mean by *Do something nostalgic*?'

'I don't know, like do something that fills me with nostalgic butterflies.'

Fran frowns at the road.

'Isn't there anything you are nostalgic for?' I ask

131

him incredulously. I don't wait for him to answer. 'I'm nostalgic over McDonald's birthday parties, and those gifts they used to give you on airplanes if you were a kid, and—' He cuts me off.

'I'm nostalgic for life not being so shitty.'

Whoa, that's dark. I clear my throat.

'Yeah, same, but pick something else, something from your childhood that you are nostalgic for.'

'I guess,' he starts carefully, 'I'm nostalgic for DVD box sets. I used to save my money and go to Walmart on Black Friday and buy a box set. Then I would binge the series and read the facts on the inserts and watch cast commentary. I miss how simple it all was. This idea of wanting something for months, trying hard to get it, and then watching it with intention. Savouring it.'

'What was your first box set?'

He cringes. '*Sex and the City.*'

'Oh, well I did think you're *such* a Miranda.'

'First of all, I've seen like five episodes but if I'm anyone I'm an Aidan. And second of all it was a gift for my mom, I saved up for her birthday.'

'I'm nostalgic for Blockbuster,' I say. 'That's where I rented box sets. We had one in my town.'

Fran smiles lightly. 'Blockbuster was the best.'

It's heartwarming to imagine a mini Fran queuing with his pocket money for the *Sex and the City* box set.

'Did she like it?'

'She loved it,' he says as if recalling the memory. 'Watched it on repeat, until Dad couldn't take it any more. Then she stopped, never watched it again.'

I wonder if those DVDs are somewhere in that house, covered in dust. Waiting.

'My mum loves Russian singers, the old kind who live for ever,' I say melancholically.

'At least she watches stuff,' says Fran and that shuts me right up.

I don't know where his mum is and I don't think he's ready to say. But I can tell it's not a happy story.

He carries that heart wound, just like me. A gash in his chest that threatens to tear and splash that pain on to the dashboard if he doesn't hold it in.

I watch the road as we pass our first ghost town.

By evening, we've passed Springfield and Tulsa. We stop at a ridiculously cheap motel that has a sign on it that says that it offers colour TV and phones. I wasn't aware black-and-white TV was still on offer anywhere. Fran asks me

133

if it's okay for him to get one room with two single beds, due to budget constraints. I agree. If he was planning on cutting me up into tiny pieces he could have done it any time while I was sleeping in his big quiet house.

When I see our room I suddenly understand why the owners of the motel thought that colour TV was a luxury worth advertising. We're faced with what can only be described as wartime cots instead of beds – covered with rough-looking wool blankets. The room has dusty, thick red curtains. And it's true there is a phone. But it has a dial on it. Even my babushka wouldn't know how to use that. The air conditioning doesn't work very well either.

I find sleep easily nonetheless.

I wake up unable to breathe. My hands are clammy, grasping at the coarse sheets, my throat dry and not letting in any air. Fran is hovering over me – it's the second time I've woken up to find myself staring into his deep brown eyes. His face is etched with concern, but I can't find it in me to be embarrassed by his closeness. I'm too exhausted by what I've just seen.

'Another nightmare?' he asks, brows creased with worry. I nod but I'm still trying to breathe. I feel a little shame creep in. In the two days that I've known this boy he has already seen me cry, have nightmares and punch someone.

He's seen me entirely. I bet it's an ugly sight.

I move away a little, pulling the harsh blanket over myself even though it's as hot as the devil's armpit. Fran gets me a Dr Pepper from the minibar. I give him a weird look.

'You really like this stuff.'

'It'll help,' he says, which makes me want to laugh. 'Dr Pepper always helps.'

'You know he's not a real doctor, right?'

I try to make light but my breathing is still hitched, my palms are wet. The can slips through my hand a little. I take a gulp. It's cold and sweet and tastes like medicine.

Fran sits down on his cot. 'It was created by a pharmacist from Texas. There's also a vanilla flavour,' he explains. He scratches the side of his face. He's still looking at me like I might cry any minute. 'Some people think it tastes like prune juice but I deeply disagree.'

'Are you trying to distract me with Dr Pepper facts?'

'I don't know, is it working?'

I try for a smile because I don't want to be the crazy crying nightmare lady. 'I'm okay. I'm fine.'

He pauses for a beat. 'No, you're not.'

That's enough to send tears rushing back.

I've been telling everyone around me that I'm fine for almost a year now and no one has ever contested it. Even when my eyes were perma-red and when things got so bad I had to schedule my tears for pre-class and lunch breaks just to relieve the permanent pressure that was built up in my face.

People would say *Are you okay?* And I would always say *I'm fine*, and they would never disagree.

That's not why they ask. They ask because they feel like they have to.

Fran can see I'm not okay. And he actually wants to know why.

Weirdly, I want to tell him, so I take a steadying breath.

'When I'm awake I'm in pain. When I'm dreaming I dream of the pain. I can't get away from it,' I say. It's a cold, black truth. The time when I should be asleep – numb, recovering – I'm still reliving it all. Again, and again, and again.

Bony fingers, hospital bed, black coffin.

The *bang* of the casket closing shut.

Bang. Bang. Bang.

'Sometimes,' I say wearily, because I know people don't like being exposed to this darkness inside of me, 'sometimes, I dream that she's alive, that she woke up in that coffin and needs help and she can't get out. On other nights I dream of the worms eating her. The worst is when I dream that it was all my fault. That if I had done something, seen the signs, made her go to a doctor earlier. They would have caught it sooner . . .'

'I'm so sorry, Nadia. I'm so sorry you feel this way.'

'You know what's even worse?' I start to shake now because what I'm about to say I've never said out loud. 'When Lizzy was sick in the later stages she messaged me and asked me to come and see her at the hospital. But I had a party to go to and seeing her like that hurt too much, so I chose the party. Because I didn't want the pain that came with seeing her. I chose a fucking party over my dying best friend. How could I do that?'

My crying turns into something deep that catches in my throat, my tears coming in wracking sobs. Fran puts his hand on my shoulder, the weight of his touch easing the pain in my chest a little.

'When I was younger,' he tells me, 'my mom was committed for a time. I was supposed to visit her weekly, and I did it one time and didn't go back. I hated the smell in that place. Hated seeing her somewhere like that. It's not pretty to feel this way, but it's normal.'

I look up at him and the tender expression on his face makes my throat ache. He squeezes my hand gently, his soft fingertips stroking my knuckles. I close my eyes, when what I really want to do is throw myself at his chest and feel his arms around me. I need a hug and I don't care who it's from. But I don't move, instead I focus on the feel of his fingers moving against mine.

'Nadia, look, life hurts us sometimes. Screw it, a lot of the time. But, the thing is, sometimes our brains take that pain and they make it worse. Way worse.'

He takes a deep breath. 'I haven't heard from my parents in eleven months. Except for the odd email. My dad is in the army. He sends me money regularly, the army pays him well, but that's about it. My mom left a while ago. She's off somewhere and I'm not sure what she's doing. They left me, and every day I wake up feeling worthless because maybe I didn't do the right thing at the right time. Maybe they would have stayed if I did something different.'

My sobs lull a little. Poor Fran. That's horrible.

'But they wouldn't have stayed. And there is nothing you could have done to have made Lizzy stay either. To have saved her.'

He stops talking and looks down at his hand on mine.

I've grabbed his and am holding it, probably a little too strongly. He releases and I pull away.

'The point is,' he continues, 'Lizzy is gone, and that's going to hurt. But don't make yourself hurt even more out of guilt. Out of the stories that your brain is trying to sell you. You did nothing wrong. Now tell me you'll try not to blame yourself any more.'

Fran seems out of breath as he opens another can of Dr Pepper and downs it.

I know he didn't want to tell me that. I know he wouldn't have normally shared something so personal. He told his story so that we could be on equal ground. I showed him a broken shard of myself, and he showed me one too.

'I'm sorry,' I say.

''Bout what?'

'Your parents. Leaving like that. And your mum, being committed.'

Fran nods but doesn't look at me.

'It's fine . . .' He avoids my gaze. 'I'm going to go check on the car.'

And just like that his walls snap back into place.

CHAPTER 9

Mocha Frappa Somethin' Somethin'

When Fran isn't back twenty minutes later I put on Larissa's fancy jacket and go to find him. He's sitting on a kerb in the parking lot staring at his Cadillac.

I sit down next to him.

'Remember I told you we were going to fix her up together?' he says. Chin jutting out at the car.

'With your dad?'

'Yeah, and when we were done we were going to take a road trip down Route 66 just like we did when I was little. Visit all the same places. When he took me to see the burros.'

'Burros?'

'Wild donkeys.'

A sadness grabs at my heart. It's not just the dead that leave us hollow and haunted, sometimes it's the living too. I clasp Fran's hand again, holding mine over his, determined not to let him wriggle free this time. Surprise flashes in his eyes then he smiles, making something hot and heavy pool into the pit of my stomach.

He doesn't let go of my hand as he shrugs his shoulders. 'I fixed her up by myself in the end. I didn't need him for it.'

'She's beautiful.' I nod my head in her direction. His gaze is intense. He briefly gnaws on his bottom lip while focusing on mine, then looks away.

'What are you out here for anyway?' I say, my throat all croaky.

The parking lot is deafening with the sound of a retreating lorry.

Fran leans in closer so I can hear him. His mouth inches from my ear, cutting over the roar of the truck, his breath warm against my cheek. I shiver, my skin breaking out in goosebumps as tiny fireworks cascade down my spine. He moves closer to me, his lips so close as he speaks that for an instant I imagine he's going to kiss my neck.

'Look up.' He points at the sky. I follow his gaze. The noisy truck pulls away, leaving us in partial darkness. Allowing me to see the massive blanket of stars.

He's grinning and now I am too. I never knew the sky could be this huge and this dark and this bright. I feel so small, while at the same time like Fran and I are standing at the centre of the universe.

Another thing on the list and I run a black line through it in my mind. Savouring it.

~~Stargazing~~.

We are sitting in the car the next day in the motel parking lot. There is a kind of air of giddiness about us. We are getting closer to our destination and we can feel it in our veins.

I know despite my message Larissa and my dad will be worried sick. But I push that feeling of guilt down, to a darker place in my mind. And I turn the key.

We head down the freeway and I force Fran to pull off at a roadside Starbucks for breakfast. He mumbles a complaint about corporate America but concedes because there is a gas station attached to it.

'I'll get this,' I say as we walk into the blissfully

air-conditioned Starbucks. He's already getting the gas, and paid for the motel, and it's the least I can do. *Literally.*

'I don't support late-stage capitalism,' he calls grumpily. I feel like Fran somehow skipped his youth and went right to the part where he yells at children to get off his lawn.

'Come on. I see you drifting at the wheel, you need a mocha frappa something something.'

'No thank you, I'll have some black gas station coffee. Plain and simple.'

'You sure you don't want a mocha frapppppaaaaa somethin' somethin'?' I coo in what must be a very annoying voice. 'With extra whipped cream on top?'

His lips twitch as he towers over me. Maybe he's not such a grumpy old man after all. My cheeks start to tingle with the realization I like making him smile.

'Whipped cream on coffee is a crime,' he says as he moves aside to wait for me by the display of sparkly water jugs and Starbucks mugs with city names on them.

I watch him as he studies the people walking in and out of the coffee shop. He's so serious yet I know it's all a front. I know deep down there's a child hidden behind that tough, stern exterior. Those tanned muscles and scary tattoos aren't fooling anyone. Not me, at least.

Suddenly, I've got an idea. I order and pay.

I stand off to the side where the drinks are delivered. The barista calls off a few names with lightning speed. Then my iced latte and egg bites for both of us. And then ...

'Unicorn Frappuccino with extra whipped cream for FRAAAAAANNY,' the barista bellows.

The barista calls out again. Fran cringes. The woman looks around and everyone else does too as if searching for the culprit. The barista checks the label irritably.

'Unicorn Frappuccino with extra whipped cream for FRAAAAAANNY.'

'Franny!' I call out, clearly looking at him. 'Get your drink.'

The barista locks eyes with him and repeats the order. Everyone is watching him. He has no choice.

He pretends not to have heard and mumbles an apology as he collects his drink and walks out.

I follow him.

We get back in the car and I slurp my drink loudly. He stares at his tower of whipped cream dubiously, as if I've gotten him a liquidized version of a rainbow. Which, to be fair, it kind of is.

I snicker.

'You're annoying, you know that?'

'I know.'

The radio is humming something familiar. My smile grows even wider when I realize they are playing the song 'San Francisco'.

I hum a little. Then I start to sing low. Then I let my voice rise.

He growls at me. '*Stop.*'

This time I bellow and turn the radio all the way up. '*IF YOU'RE GOING TO SAAAN FRANCISCO.*'

'Please make it stop.

'...*FLOWERS IN YOUR HAIR.*'

Fran turns the radio down.

I laugh, and the sharp nature of my laugh terrifies me. I sound like Gollum in his cave.

I sound as if I haven't laughed in months. Maybe I haven't.

It feels good and I'm laughing all the way from my belly as I belt out the rest of the words to the song.

I turn it all the way up again as Fran joins the freeway. He's scowling, but as his warm brown eyes meet mine he finally smiles and I grin back in return.

He drinks his entire frap to the dregs.

*

We keep driving. Past deserted gas stations, past more ghost towns and more quirky shopping stops.

'So,' Fran announces, one hand on the wheel. 'What was Lizzy like? What was she into?'

'She liked Comic Cons, fantasy series, *Star Wars*, that kind of stuff.'

'*Star Wars* is a classic.'

'I wouldn't know, I've never seen them, and now I feel kind of bad because Lizzy was into all of it . . .'

There's a moment of silence and then all of a sudden, as if it just dawned on him, Fran thunders, 'YOU'VE NEVER SEEN *STAR WARS*?'

'Nope.' I shrug. *So what?*

'Why didn't Lizzy watch it with you?'

'We mostly spent our time re-watching *Gilmore Girls*.'

Fran changes lanes. He seems perplexed.

'Why would you ever re-watch a show? I mean once, okay, but more than that is a pass,' he says, and I swear he's speaking Mandarin.

'Okay, so you like Dr Pepper, right?'

His eyes dart to me. Then turn back to the freeway.

'Yeah.'

'But you've tasted it already, why keep tasting it?'

'Because it's the best taste in the world.'

'*Gilmore Girls* is the television equivalent of a Dr Pepper.'

I've clearly made Fran thirsty because in the next town he pulls up at a gas station for some Dr Pepper.

'I need to wash away the taste of that fairy blood cocktail you got me,' he declares. I laugh.

I get out to stretch my legs and wait for him. God it's freaking hot. How do people live out here? The gas station is old and peculiar. It looks more like a white suburban house with multiple garages and a slanted green roof, very different from the service stations I'm used to back in Slough. I guess this is what vintage Americana stations look like.

Someone has gone to great lengths to restore the old pumps and cover them in a fresh coat of Coca-Cola-red paint. Despite all the effort, the quaint old-timey station already shows signs of being run down by the dust and wind and sun. The pumps are dull and scratched as if by animal claws, the building weathered, the paint on the garage doors peeling, revealing rust underneath.

Something black moves out of the corner of my eye and for a terrifying second, I think it's a person reaching for me. But it's not. It's a procession of cars passing us at a crawl, much slower than cars normally go. Especially on a deserted road like this.

My mind blanks. It's a hearse. A death display. Moving at a crawl so that everyone knows they are mourning. I can see the coffin in the back window, so clear and dark against the sun-blanched desert.

I can't stop staring at it, everything around me turning fuzzy so all I see is the box containing a dead person. My breath quickens, my hands cold but sweaty.

None of this is natural. All of it is wrong.

A car is following the hearse with a family inside. I can see their faces. I can see Lizzy's family's faces in them all. Her parents. The way her mother howled with pain inside that church.

I remember the coffin that held Lizzy. The ribbons and the eggshell silk that was all so futile and just screamed death.

Death, death, death.

I remember collapsing knees first in the snow. So white and pure, rare for the UK, the black coffin was stark against it.

I stumble back, away, nausea ripping through me. I can't breathe. I'm going to collapse right here on the scalding pavement, the sight of that family merging into Lizzy's in my mind.

'Nadia!' Fran's voice is distant and murky. As if I'm

hearing him through water. My throat is closing. This is it. Nothing will ever be okay again.

'Breathe,' I hear him say in the distance. 'Nadia.' His hands are on my shoulders as I buckle. He comes down with me, sinking to my level, eyes boring into mine as a I heave. Vomit rises and my stomach drops down. *Breathe, breathe, breathe.* I don't know if it's my own internal voice or if it's Fran saying this.

'You're having a panic attack,' he says. His brown eyes are gentle. He looks frightened, like he's found a baby bird with a wounded wing. I try to focus on him. On the tattoos on his arms, homing in on Captain Crunch.

'Breathe.' He says it again as if it were a long word like an exhale. 'Just breathe. That's all you got to do right now. Can you do that for me, Nadia?'

He's not letting go of my shoulders and the world refocuses a little. I push that hearse away, down into the pits of my mind. I never want to see another one of those cursed cars again.

'It's gone,' he says warmly. His eyes search mine again.

My breathing is slowing but I'm so exhausted that I feel like I just ran a marathon.

'It's gone,' he repeats, 'and it's not coming back.'

'Okay,' I manage. My voice is a croak.

Fran holds a cold can against my forehead. It feels good.

We sit there for a minute. His one hand stays on my shoulder, the other holds the can in place.

I breathe. That's all I can do.

We sit together quietly as I try not to think about the emptiness inside of me that seems to be expanding.

I'm haunted like those ghost towns.

I'm hollow inside.

CHAPTER 10

Two birds, one Gosling

I frown. 'What are we doing here?'

It's not long after lunch and we've stopped again. At this point we won't arrive in LA till next year.

Fran pulls the car slightly off-road, rocks skittering from the tyres as if they're fleeing us. The beams of sun are searing and I'm over the idea of how Instagrammable everything in the desert is. It's hot and dead and deadly.

We seem to be parked by a patch of desert, next to a small road that leads to a few abandoned buildings.

'Getting another thing off the list,' he says as he gets out of the car.

I scramble to follow him.

'Why are you so into this list?'

He sighs but keeps walking. 'Very little in life is simple; this list is simple. You just check things off. I guess I kind of like that.'

I bite back my retort; nothing about Lizzy's list is simple. But Fran seems to think that he's on some holy mission to help me get it done.

'And what do these abandoned houses have to do with the list?'

'You said you're afraid of ghosts,' says Fran, kicking up some dirt. 'And maybe it would even be a fair assumption to say you're scared shitless of them.'

I stall, and throw a distrustful look at the cluster of abandoned buildings. I always thought ghost towns were old abandoned western towns – untouched, left behind from the gold rush days. With saloons and swinging doors and tiny jails that spelled the word Sheriff. Turns out many ghost towns along Route 66 are just regular towns from more recent times, left behind to rot when their inhabitants died or moved on looking for work. They are morbid, sad, decrepit things.

I glance up and down the street. We could be anywhere,

which makes it even weirder, like we've stepped into a zombie apocalypse.

I make out what was once a café and a storefront and a bunch of clapboard houses, their once-white paint grey and peeling. The front yards are full of weeds, now dry and yellowing; some even have the rusty remains of what used to be garden furniture. Did everyone just up and leave together? Or was it bit by bit, until just one lonely couple was left clinging on to a time and place that had no future?

I try not to think about it. About who lived here. About how many have died.

'A quick walk around, I promise. Just enough for you to feel that ripple of fear on your skin.'

I frown some more but follow him towards the buildings. I take care to shuffle my feet. I read somewhere that snakes can feel vibrations and they stay away from them.

We enter the first building. It feels wrong, as if we're breaking into someone's home. There is nothing special but a rusted fridge and lot of broken wood and corroded nails. It's like navigating a minefield of tetanus.

'*Who you gonna call?*' Fran shouts. He thinks he's hilarious. He follows it up with a whistle.

I don't give him the satisfaction of saying *Ghost Busters!* Even though I really, really want to.

We walk through a few rooms and there is nothing to see. The building doesn't even have a roof. It's not scary. It's depressing.

I feel a drop on my forehead and I shriek.

My first thought is *ghost blood.*

Get a grip, Nadia, ghosts don't bleed. My second thought is even weirder. *Rain.*

'Whoa,' says Fran. He looks up at the purple-grey sky through the gash in the ceiling with utter disbelief. 'That's pretty rare.'

'Let's go back to the car,' I groan. Things crunch beneath my feet. I hate it here. There's a broken bed, and clothing has been left behind. Why are abandoned places always littered with half-heartedly discarded possessions? In the rust-covered bathroom there's half a tube of used toothpaste and hung towels up, ready to use. A place frozen in time, like the inhabitants were beamed up by aliens.

What used to be the bedroom is littered with clothes, half on the floor and bed, half hung up intact in the armoire, as if the inhabitants would come back any minute. Or as if the residents fled, with no time to pack.

Or worse, they went somewhere where you don't need a suitcase.

Everything about this place screams death. Instead of a box, this entire town is a coffin.

Even all the plants that have tried to slither their way in through the many openings of the house have mostly died and shrivelled up. Probably found the house too depressing.

'I want to leave,' I say, following Fran into a creepy living room. It's dark and dusty, I can hear things skittering about. There's an ancient boxy TV.

'Why, are you ... *scared*?' Fran asks, gleefully. 'Need me to hold your hand?'

God, he really is obsessed with the list.

'Actually, no not at all, I just find it depressing. A house that used to be full of people. Now it's a shell. Full of silence where there used to be voices.'

I think I'm being poetic but something dark crosses his features and I bite my lip. I hope he doesn't think I was referring to his house too.

'No, you're checking this off your list. Number 4 – *Do something that scares you.* Don't be a coward.'

'A coward?' I repeat, flabbergasted. I tiptoe after him as he changes rooms. I navigate around rusty nails, trying my best to avoid their jagged tips.

'A coward?'

I'm halfway around the world, with a boy, in a ghost house, in a ghost town, I'm not a coward!

'But you're not scared,' he says simply.

'Doesn't that make me the opposite of a coward?'

'No, not being scared is not what makes you brave. Being scared and facing it is bravery.'

'So, it's my fault this carcass of a house doesn't scare me?'

'You need to give it one hundred per cent.'

What does that even mean?

'Surrender to your fear,' he adds.

His expression infuriates me. He thinks it's so easy. Easy to knock things from the list. Easy to forget Lizzy and move on. Easy to be brave. It starts to rain harder. We are standing right under the massive hole in the ceiling and my face is getting damp.

'You have no business telling me how to be brave,' I mumble. He looks genuinely surprised.

'Why not?'

I sidestep a pile of rubble and wipe rainwater from my face. 'Because, Fran, maybe *you* have no idea how to be brave either. You don't have any more of an idea than I do.

'What have you done recently that made you give in to

your fear?' I continue, indignation and rage rising up in me. 'Huh? You keep giving me these lectures about seizing the day, and finishing this god-forsaken list, and seizing life by the balls or the hooves or the horns or whatever. This list is *not* easy and it won't bring Lizzy back.'

The rain is falling harder and we're both already soaked. Fran's T-shirt is clinging to his chest, his hair plastered to his face, a drop of water working its way down his cheek. I push my wet hair back from my face.

'And when is the last time you did something that scared you, huh? How about you try it. Do something that isn't you! That is outside your comfort zone. YOU can't even get a coffee at Starbucks!'

Fran isn't moving, he's just staring at me as I lay into him, rain running down his face. I have water in my eyes too but I'm too angry, too charged, to wipe it away. He's been pushing and pushing me since we got here and now he's got his reaction. His jaw is tense, every inch of his body rigid like he wants to lash out or storm off. Waiting for him to reply is like waiting for the lightning during a storm.

I hold my ground. The rage feels good once it starts pouring from me like a superpower. I could bring this spectral house down with my rage.

'FINE,' he thunders. 'You want me to do something outside of my comfort zone? Something that scares me?'

'THAT WOULD BE NICE!' I thunder back.

He crosses the space between us. The floorboards shriek in answer, and I shrink back a little.

The rain is falling so hard now I can't see him clearly, but I feel his touch as he cups my face in his hands. His skin is warm against my cold cheeks, water from his hair dripping on to mine as he leans closer. My body moves on its own, my mind completely blank. I tilt my chin up and go to say something, but as my lips part he brings his mouth down on mine.

His hands are in my hair, his chest hard against me. Every part of me melts.

Fran deepens the kiss and I feel him leaning me back. It's the dip at the end of a tango, it's the train station goodbye kiss, it's the beat peaking in a Shawn Next song.

Everything disappears. The ghost town, the pain, the bad memories – right now all I am is what I'm feeling and I'm floating, and safe, and everything is perfect.

He lets me go and I straighten up. Breathless.

Frans wipes the rain from his mouth and the feel of my lips from his. I try not to take it personally. We're both soaked. I stare at him, his brown-black eyes looking at me through sopping lashes. He looks intent, then the seriousness of it all evaporates and he smiles lightly. Like he has a secret.

'Whatchadothatfor?' My words blend together because I'm still breathless. The sharp whip of lightning and the distant roll of thunder booms in the distance.

'You told me to do something that scares me, and I did. Because being cheesy scares me. And kissing someone like I'm in some kind of romcom remake is very far outside of my comfort zone,' he says. His smile widens to a cheeky grin.

Cheesy? That absolute jerk.

I don't say anything as understanding slithers into me. Past the breathlessness. Past the exhilaration of the kiss.

'You want me to cross the kiss off my list,' I say.

'Two birds, one Gosling.'

He winks at me and exits the building.

He's so arrogant. I wipe my mouth with the back of my hand and spit on the floor like a sailor.

What was that sound?

I'm worried that the ghost building's structure won't hold. It will crumble under my feet and swallow me up into the desert. There might be rattlesnakes under the floorboards; I can almost hear their tails. Thunder rumbles again and, fear coursing through me, I decide I'll be stubborn when it doesn't mean risking my life.

'That kiss doesn't count,' I yell after him. 'For a Gosling kiss the other person has to be smitten!'

I hurry after him, leaving the ghosts behind us.

CHAPTER 11

One-way ticket to Uranus

'This is where we stock up,' says Fran. I get out of the car and follow his gaze to another weird building, another roadside attraction. *The Uranus Candy Factory.*

I'm still annoyed from the surprise trick Gosling kiss a few hours ago. But I'm not going to show him that. I'm also annoyed because I don't know whether he just kissed me to prove a point. Did he want to kiss me? Or was he just forcing me to check something off Lizzy's list? I'm not going to. It doesn't count and I'll be damned if I skip the funnest thing on the list just because Fran is cocky.

'What are we stocking up on?'

'On candy.'

Eat sweets for dinner.

'I'm not sure every point on the list is literal,' I lie, reluctantly following him into the general store. Lizzy loved overeating sweets, spreading them out on her duvet like treasure, but I'm hungry for some normal food.

'Nah, I'm pretty sure it's very literal,' says Fran with a conspiratorial look as he pushes through the glass door.

The general store is pretty amazing. They have wicker baskets stocked to the brim with colourful fudge. They have hand-dipped caramel apples, sprinkle-covered bars of fudge the flavour of 'birthday cake', alien-themed candy and caramelized nuts in every shape and size. The cavernous space is littered with weird statues, bits of neon signage and selections of tinned novelty mints.

There are also more anus puns than I think *anyone* would deem acceptable.

Fran puts a hand on my waist to move past me and into a tight space by the lollipop display. My stomach does an annoying little flip.

'So.' I clear my throat, browsing a rack of cleverly named candies. I examine a Milk Chocolate from Uranus candy bar. 'Where were your parents the last time you heard from them?'

I know that's a bit blunt but Fran hasn't exactly been holding back on asking me questions about me and Lizzy or forcing me into uncomfortable situations. He looks at the fudge in the glass display.

'My dad is on his second tour in the Middle East; he chose not to take his last leave,' he says casually. 'We spoke a few months ago via Zoom.' He grabs a shopping basket and throws in a cone-shaped pack of candied pecans.

I gulp but try not to let my emotions show on my face. My parents are distant and have no room for my pain, and they think mental health is an expression made up by Western marketing companies, but I can't imagine them choosing not to see me. That seems to be what Fran's dad did; he point-blank chose more time in a war zone over seeing his own son.

'And has your dad seen your mum?'

'Not exactly.'

What the hell does that mean?

Getting information out of Fran is like manual labour. You have to keep digging.

I examine a lollipop shaped like an alien's head. I throw it in the basket 'cause why not?

163

'So, what's the real reason you wanted to drive me to LA? I know it's not because you need a holiday or wanted to see Route 66.'

I don't look at him. I pretend to examine another candy, in case my gaze throws him off. He waits for me to look up as if he knows exactly what I'm trying to do.

Fran picks up a large packet of individually wrapped pieces of purple lavender-flavored fudge and demonstratively plops it into the wicker carrier basket.

'We are here to get enough candy to make you sick, we are not here for a therapy session.'

I stick my tongue out at him.

CHAPTER 12

Someone is someone else's father

We put a few more hours of driving under our belt and then check into our second motel. Tomorrow is our last full day on the road before we reach Los Angeles. I turn my internet on, ignoring the barrage of incoming messages, and send another round of *I'm safe. I'm sorry. I'll be back soon.* I shriek and throw aside my phone when I see a message in all caps arrive from my mum. *She knows.* I swipe away from the notifications and switch to airplane mode, tossing my phone into my bag as if I'm hiding it from myself.

I realize that I'm like a child delaying the inevitable

repercussions. But existing in this temporary bubble, in this temporary madness, with Fran feels good. Ticking things off Lizzy's list feels good too, as if purpose were something bubbling up inside of me. Rising.

The moment I face the music I'll be back to reality.

Despite all the fun, I've felt awkward around Fran ever since he kissed me. Awkward enough to brush my teeth and brush my hair way before bedtime when he leaves me in the simple room and says he has to go get something.

I have absolutely no idea what to do with my body; my hands cross over then uncross. I realize it's absolutely ridiculous to feel this way just because we have a shared room, and just because he kissed me to prove a point. I look in the mirror and try to kind of flip my hair back and forth before it settles. It's brown and wavy and boring and I kind of wish I had a more Slavic look. But my family comes from the far east of Russia. A place famous for its poppy fields and the sadness such a pretty flower can bring. None of us have blue eyes or hair the colour of wheat. There's a knock on the door and I open it.

There is a red stick hanging from Fran's mouth. His hands are full of more candy.

'Seriously?'

He pushes past me into the room and dumps the contents on the questionable floral bedspread.

'Dinner is served,' he announces.

'What's in your mouth?'

'Huh?' He tugs the strand from his mouth. 'Red Vine.' He says it like it's the most obvious thing in the world. 'I couldn't let you dine on candy without including Red Vines in the mix.'

'I've never tried one.'

He hands me a Red Vine. It tastes like candle wax.

'That's not all, I have something else,' he announces cryptically. He seems excited. Seeing brooding Fran giddy is *very* weird.

He heads back out and returns a few seconds later, waving a couple of VHS tapes at me.

'This motel has a VHS library. Can you believe it? And I have found *Star Wars* parts IV and V. Which means . . .' Fran walks over to the ratty VHS player on our colour TV. He pops the first one in. The only reason I know what the bulky taper is, and how to use it, is because my grandmother insists on keeping her ancient VHS player.

'You *will* watch *Star Wars*,' Fran continues. 'While *eating candy for dinner*, while *doing something nostalgic*.'

He points at the VHS player. 'Two things off the list, I'm a freaking genius!'

This time I smile. Even though I think his obsession with the list is weird, eating candies and watching a movie is something I can handle.

We eat through our Uranus loot and watch the first part of *Star Wars*. Fran is intent the entire time, as if he hasn't seen it before. But sometimes I see his lips moving as he recites the lines he knows by heart. I will myself to look away from his lips.

We take a break between the first film and the second film.

'You really like *Star Wars*.'

'It means a lot to me,' he says. 'My best friend and I used to ride our BMX bikes to this outdoor theatre and watch *Star Wars* there in the summertime. We didn't pay the cover charge, just snuck in.'

Something about the way he says *best friend* reminds me of the way I say Lizzy's name.

But no, there's something else too.

Riding BMX bikes with my best friend.

I've heard that somewhere. It's familiar. Fran bends over to put the second VHS into the player. I gasp when I put two and two together.

Shawn Next used to ride BMX bikes with his best friend who lived on his street! It's in the biography.

'You were Shawn Next's best friend,' I say.

Fran turns around, pale with shock.

'Oh my God you were,' I gasp again because one gasp just doesn't seem like enough.

'Can we just drop this?'

I squeal. 'No, we absolutely cannot. Is that why you're going to LA with me? To see your best friend?'

This whole time I just thought he had like a forwarding address or something. Not that he was his best friend. I can't freaking believe it.

'He's no longer my best friend,' says Fran.

'How come?'

'*How come?*' Fran repeats incredulously. 'Because some crazed fans ambushed his house and he had to move and I never heard from him again.'

Oh.

'Like, never again?' I instantly regret asking because Fran looks so sad. But he's annoyed when he finally answers me.

'No, never.'

I don't really know what to say. It sucks that his best friend got famous and moved away and they never spoke again. It sucks that his parents must have left shortly after. I want to reach out and hug Fran but I know that's not what he needs or wants.

'I don't want to talk about it any more,' he warns.

I nod, he puts the film on, and I try to focus on the flying spaceships, but all I think about is that Fran used to be Shawn Next's best friend, and then Shawn Next just abandoned him. Forgot about him overnight.

I'm not sure how that makes me feel about my pop idol. I keep eating candy and thinking about it.

Midway through the movie my stomach begins to hurt. Like a lot.

I get to the toilet and heave. Candy chunks come flying out of me.

My vomit is sickly sweet. I really did overdo it. I heave again.

I hear Fran chuckle from the bedroom. Then he does a Yoda impression.

'Eat less candy you must, young Padawan.'

'Oh, shut up!' I call back. 'This is your fault.'

By the time I make it into my bed, I'm drenched with sweat and mortified. The same boy who kissed me a few hours prior has now listened to me vomit.

I tuck myself into my bed. The film is still on. I've

lost track of who killed whom and why and what they all want.

'Switch it off,' I mumble grumpily. The sound of firing blasters and colliding lightsabers is giving me a headache.

'But it's the best part,' Fran complains. 'You will miss the ending.'

'I already know how it ends.'

'Oh yeah?' He rolls his eyes. 'How?'

I turn on my side, feeling half asleep already. 'Someone is someone else's father.'

CHAPTER 13

A big ball of fur

For breakfast we buy bagels stuffed with a thick layer of cold cream cheese, and mini powdered doughnuts that make your whole mouth and face white, and we pair them with Fran's favourite – black gas-station coffee.

'This stuff burns your throat on the way in,' I complain, fitting my scalding cup into the cup holder.

'Yeah, but it will get you wired like no other coffee ever could. Definitely no fluffy unicorn frapawhatever.'

Fran takes a luxurious swig of coffee as he pulls on to the freeway. I watch his lips close over the rim of the plastic lid, his strong hands holding on to the cup, and

I remember the feel of his lips on mine and how safe I felt in his arms. I push the thought away. It was all pretend. He just did it to prove a point. To get something off the list, because he's stubborn and competitive.

I tear my gaze away from him and focus on the open road.

Sure, he's a good kisser. The best I have ever kissed to be honest. But then he's competing against awkward Roma in the bushes in fourth form, and drunken Anwar behind a Tesco car park after Lizzy's birthday party. And fumbling Charles. That's not a lot of competition.

'This nectar,' he gestures at the cup, 'could help you stay awake an entire night.'

'Why would you want to stay awake an entire night?'

Fran's face falls and I instantly regret asking.

'My mom would disappear sometimes. My dad and I would go looking for her at night. He would buy us black coffees to keep us alert, wired. The habit kind of stuck.'

'Oh,' I say, blinking hard so he can't see my reaction.

My chest aches with the image of a young Fran drinking nasty gas-station coffee, sitting beside his father as they drove through busy parking lots at night looking for his mother. He must have been so scared, that mix of anxiety and hope as he eagerly scanned the streets, chugging back cheap caffeine to stay alert when he should have been tucked up safely in bed knowing his mother was in the next room if he needed her.

I let the silence linger for a little because I don't know what to say. After a while, I clear my throat.

'Your mum been unwell a long time?'

Fran nods sombrely. He turns the radio up. The conversation is closed. I take the hint and focus back on the road. I'm not sure what it would take for him to open up. I'm not sure why I want him to either.

A few pop ballads keep us company, until the radio host talks about Shawn Next's upcoming LA concert, and follows it up with his latest song, 'Too Good to Love Me'.

'Who do you think this song is about?' I ask.

'I don't know, one of his many girlfriends.'

Shawn has had an impressive line-up of girlfriends over the years. Models, actresses, influencers. Lizzy and I used to look up who he was dating on gossip socials and hate on them. Very anti-feminist of us, I'll admit.

'Do you think Shawn ever wrote a song about you?'

Fran cringes.

'We were friends, not lovers.'

'People write songs about friends. I write poems about Lizzy all the time.'

'It's not the same.'

'How is it not the same?'

'He hasn't written any songs about me, okay? Just drop it,' Fran snaps.

'Okay, okay,' I mutter. 'I'm sorry.'

The silence that stretches after Fran's outburst is long and tense. I shouldn't have pushed him, not about his mother, not about Shawn. After nearly an hour of silence we pull up to what looks like another ghost town. I can tell Fran is still grumpy.

'What are we doing here?' I say, following him out of the car.

'Getting another thing off your list,' he says.

It's nice that he wants to help me but that doesn't mean I should have to deal with his sullenness. I never asked him to help me get through the list. That was his own decision. And now I need to deal with his pushiness and bad moods?

'I can finish the list another time. We don't have to obsess over it.'

'Don't you *want* to finish it? Don't you want closure?' His tone is venomous.

'Don't judge me,' I say, hurt.

'Do you know what some people would give for closure? And you've got it right there on a list, a detailed to-do list of exactly how you can get there, and you refuse to do it!'

I don't know if Fran's aware that his voice is rising with every word.

He's yelling at me, and I've done nothing wrong.

'Maybe I don't want closure!' I yell back. 'It won't bring her back. Or stop the pain. What's the freaking point?'

'You don't want closure because you're afraid of it.'

My stomach sinks. 'You know what? Screw you, Fran!'

I storm off angrily. Past another cheesy gift shop, I weave through a bunch of tourists. This ghost town seems to be a lot more popular than the rest. Tears are hot on my face and I don't stop walking. I just keep marching on angrily, banking left behind a wooden shack. I come to a standstill, arms crossed, crying angrily. How dare he lecture me on closure.

I've got too much pride to admit that I want his help, but I'm also embarrassed that all I seem to do in front of this boy who's travelling across three states for me is cry. Knocking a few things off the list after months of paralysis felt good. Really good. But maybe Fran's right and I'm afraid to finish. Afraid to see what's on the other side. And Fran kissing me has only made everything more confusing. Why is he so bent on helping me complete this thing? Does he just pity me?

Someone nudges me in the shoulder.

'Leave me alone, Fran!'

He nudges me again, hard. I whip around.

'I SAID LEAVE ME ...' My voice fades away as I come face to face with a donkey.

For a moment we just stare at each other. His kind black eyes boring into mine. Are donkeys dangerous?

'You shouldn't yell at the donkey, he didn't do anything wrong,' says a voice behind him. I pet the donkey on the head and follow Fran out from behind the shack, surprised to find the small ghost town is full of donkeys now.

'It's a donkey town,' he explains.

'This isn't on the list,' I say.

Fran rocks back and forth on his heels. 'No. But it is on mine. My dad brought me here once when I was little, I've always wanted to come back, and I figured cuddling some cute animals could help you too. Are you still mad?'

'I'll let you know after I cuddle some donkeys,' I say, smiling over my shoulder.

*

177

I'm one hundred per cent not mad any more, mostly because I'm having a lot of fun. We walk around the town, watching fake cowboys re-enact dramatic duels in the town centre. Fran and I giggle as one of the cowboys sinks to his knees and screams *God why me?* to the heavens before falling flat on his face.

We play county fair-style games, browse the quirky gift shop, which features oddities like Donkey Butter soap, and we buy the special food that we are allowed to feed the donkeys. I make it my mission to scratch the ears of each donkey I meet, and to feed them all as well.

I only take a short break from donkey snuggles when I desperately need to pee.

When I emerge from the ladies' room Fran is standing there waiting for me, holding a stuffed donkey in his hands. He's looking at me strangely, a mix of confusion, shyness and amusement crossing his features.

'I won this,' he says, awkwardly. 'You should have it.'

He half shoves it at me and I take it. His fingers brush against mine and he snatches his hand away.

'What game did you win?' I ask, my voice sounding strained.

'One of those dart balloon piercing games.'

He's looking at his shoes, kicking a stone along the dirt floor. I focus on the cuddly toy.

'Aww, he's so cute.' I look adoringly into his big black plastic eyes. 'I'm going to name him Pushok.'

'What does that mean?'

'Means ball of fur.'

'Five points for originality,' he says approvingly. 'You know these donkeys are actually called *burros*,' he adds.

'Burros.' I taste the word. 'What does that mean?'

'Means *donkey* in Spanish.'

I reach out and pet the donkey nearest to me. His fur feels oily and soft and wonderful. He sniffs at my jean pockets. I squeal when a baby burro knocks my knee. It has a big sticker on its forehead that says DON'T FEED ME. Probably because it's a baby and still reliant on its mother's milk.

Fran and I turn to one another at the same time and he gives me a shy smile that makes my stomach flip.

By the time we make it back to the car I'm smiling ear to ear. Holding Pushok close to me.

Wait a minute. I side-eye Fran, giving him a mischievous look.

'The top prize at the dart stand is a tub of slime,' I say teasingly. 'Not a soft toy.'

Fran looks anywhere but at me as he struggles to open his car door. He shrugs his shoulders.

'I bought it, so what?'

He bought me a gift?

'Why did you lie?'

'I don't . . .' He pauses as he finally succeeds in opening the car door. A definite blush is creeping up his tanned checks. 'I don't know. I just wanted to see you smile, okay? I didn't want you to be sad any more. And I was awful earlier.' Fran unlocks my door from the inside and starts the engine, but I just stand there, confused, derailed by his comment. *He just wanted to see me smile.*

I think about this as we drive away from the donkey ghost town. Fran just wanted to make me happy. It's such a simple thing, but it seems so alien since Lizzy died. I realize suddenly that it's all I've been wanting from my family, for them to notice that I'm this sad and be worried about it. I didn't want Mum's lectures about how there are children starving in the world and I'm refusing to eat. I wanted her to understand that I was refusing to eat because it reminded me of watching Lizzy struggle with the mush they fed her. For weeks, food made me think of cancer and death and I didn't want any of it. I wanted to be as empty as I felt. I didn't need my family to change

180

me, I just wanted them to accept my sadness and to care how much I was hurting. I hug Pushok tighter to my chest.

He just wanted to see me smile.

Fran speeds up on the highway.

'LA here we come,' I announce to no one in particular.

Fran nods. 'We just have one stop left.'

CHAPTER 14

Royal Dansk cookies

'Does your grandma—' I start.

'*Abuela*,' he corrects. Smiling at the open road beyond the dash.

'Abuela,' I continue. 'Does she have a chequered bag on wheels for shopping?'

'Of course,' he says. 'Does yours have fifteen pairs of house shoes?'

'Yes.' I sip my latest Slurpee creation – blue raspberry mixed with Sour Patch Kids' tropical paradise. 'We call them *tapochki*.'

'Hmm,' Fran tuts. 'No point for either of us. But I think I have a good one. Did your grandma—'

'*Babushka*,' I correct him.

'Fine.' Fran rolls his eyes but smiles. 'Did your babushka ever use said house shoes as a weapon to chase you with when you were in trouble?'

'One of them did. One hundred per cent. No point for you. *Oohh*, I have a good one. Did your grandma keep all of her sewing supplies in a cookie tin?'

'Royal Dansk cookies.'

'Exactly!' I yelp, nearly spilling my Slurpee over my lap. 'The sheer amount of disappointment I felt each time I thought it was a new tin and I could have the sugar-dusted round cookie just to find it was yet more sewing equipment.'

Fran laughs. 'No point for you.'

Over the course of our drive Fran and I have developed a weird sort of game. We name stereotypical immigrant things our grandmas do and if they both do it we don't get a point. Fran has won the last two rounds.

'Does your grandma watch Latin American soap operas and yell at the screen?' he fires back.

'Mostly Turkish ones, but there were a few Colombian ones,' I say, crossing my legs. 'And you can say *telenovela*. Everybody knows that word.'

'It's your turn.'

'Dog-hair socks.'

His eyes widen and he makes a face that makes me laugh. 'Excuse me?'

'Socks knitted from collected dog hair. Meant to take away any cold or flu.'

Fran laughs. 'Though my abuela would be obsessed with me wearing socks; every abuela knows the fastest way of getting ill is going barefoot. But I can't say I've ever been given dog-hair socks. Sadly.' He laughs again.

'My point!' I yell triumphantly.

'Does your babushka wear one of those colourful headscarves?' Fran asks.

'When it's cold, yeah.'

'Huh, turns out some stereotypes are true,' he says.

'You know what I hate?' I say suddenly. 'I hate that in movies Russians are always villains, cleaners or sex workers. Always.'

'We get the villains and cleaners treatment too,' he counters.

'Can we get some other roles too?' I complain, slurping up the last few bits of my concoction.

Fran nods. 'And I'm sick of Spanglish in films.'

'When we get to LA we should tell the big studios to

stop being so lazy. They can hire us as consultants,' I say. Fran laughs again.

'Hey.' I nudge him. 'If you don't mind me asking, where is your abuela?'

Fran's expression sobers. The laughter dies out.

'My grandma moved to Connecticut to be closer to my dad's brother. Because his kids are a lot younger than me.'

His mum, his dad, his grandma, how many people decided to up and leave Fran? Did anyone stop to think how he was getting on?

'Have you thought about moving closer to her?'

'I've thought about it, that's one of the reasons I want to go to NYU.'

'I've heard that's a great school,' I say for lack of anything better to say. Being next to his grandmother would be a massive bonus. 'Do you think you will get in?'

'I have the grades. But, they don't look favourably on community college transfers. I also have a record. Over a fight.'

'What was the fight over?'

'I wouldn't call it a fight. My neighbours down the street called ICE on me. That's our immigration police,' he clarifies. I knew that from the movies but I nod along so he continues. 'Even though I was born here. Even though they knew me since I was little. When they saw my parents weren't around any more, they called ICE. Not even child services, just immigration. When they arrived I resisted arrest.'

I stare at him, horrified. 'That's awful, Fran. I'm so sorry.'

'Yeah well. If you don't have any immigration authority stories then I win another point.' I can tell he's trying to lighten the conversation but the air in the car is suddenly heavy and serious.

I finish my Slurpee and shiver at the cold settling in my stomach.

'Nothing like that, you win,' I say. 'All the rounds. I owe you a glazed doughnut.'

'How about we stop for a full meal? We've been eating like feral raccoons the entire trip.' Fran smiles at me.

'That would be nice.'

We stop at a barbecue place outside a large grocery store, and I treat Fran to ribs, mac and cheese, and the most delicious coleslaw I've ever tried.

'You were right,' I tell him, tugging the last bit of sweet meat from the bone. 'The raccoon lifestyle isn't for me.'

'No more candy dinners?' says Fran, wriggling his

thick brows as he polishes off the last bit of bacon in his mac and cheese tray.

I think of the Uranus Fudge I had for dinner and nearly lose my food all over again. 'No, not for me. Does your dad barbecue?' I ask.

Fran shakes his head as he puts the contents of our trays in the rubbish bin, careful to separate the plastic. 'But Shawn's dad did. Brisket. Hot dogs on summer days.'

I smile when Fran's back is to me as he heads towards the grocery store. These morsels of his and Shawn's story that he keeps feeding me are tiny, but special. As if bits of their friendship were crystallized in them. They carry the same warm weight that mine and Lizzy's stories do.

'Let's buy some healthy – ish – snacks for our last night on the road,' he says as I follow him through the sliding doors and past the whiplash of icy air con.

'What are you doing?' Fran asks as he tries to focus on the road. It's been a few hours since the barbecue and we've moved on to playing the grandpa version of the previous game.

'I'm having a snack?' I say, lifting my bread in the air.

'Onions.' Fran seems shocked. 'Onions on bread?'

'Umm, it's spring onions, with rye and butter and . . .' I shake the small circular packet at him. I bought the onions and rye, then secured a small butter packet and plastic knife at the deli stand.

'Oh, and salt,' I add. 'AKA a healthy quick snack. You're the one who criticized our eating habits. *Here.* Vitamins.' I hand him a spring onion. 'Just bite into it.'

Fran hesitates and then takes a crunchy bite. His expression turns sour. I give him some rye with butter and salt on it. 'Now chase with this.'

He obeys and his expression softens a little.

'See? Spring onions are the most delicious snack. My grandma has made this snack for me since I was little.'

'Hmmm.' Fran keeps chewing with a dubious expression. 'It grows on you.'

'Liar,' I laugh.

'Remind me to show you chilli on mango,' he says.

I nod, marvelling at how we've settled into a routine of making plans, as if we might stay friends. As if we might stay in this moment for ever.

'You should text your family, they are probably worried sick,' he says and it breaks the spell.

My phone in my pocket, back on airplane mode, is a

stark reminder that there's a real world out there in which I'm in heaps of trouble.

I pull it out gingerly and engage in the same ritual of sending them all a quick-fire message confirming my safety and my imminent return. My eyes linger on a notification from my mum that I wasn't fast enough to swipe away.

HOW CAN YOU BE THIS SELFISH?

I tuck the phone away.

A shudder runs through me at the thought of my parents' reaction when I get back and explain I was on a wild goose chase across America. I vow to record a full audio for Dad when we hit LA. Hearing my voice might appease them, that I'm safe . . . even if a little unhinged.

We continue in companionable silence, the radio playing some old country song, the sun beating through the windshield on to my bare legs. Then the desert scenery begins to transform before my eyes. Suddenly the sparse dusty plains give way to towering red mountains

'What is that?' I cry out.

Fran shakes his head like I'm crazy.

'You never seen a canyon before?'

I give him a playful dig. He knows I've never seen a canyon before; it's not like I have one on my local high street back at home.

He reaches out and tips my chin up with a chuckle. I had no idea my mouth was gaping open.

'This is . . .' I don't have words for what I'm seeing. Reds, oranges and yellows blend together, jumping out against the bright blue sky.

Fran is grinning. 'I know.'

And though for a millisecond my brain tries to remind me that Lizzy will never get to see any of this, I manage to shut it out this time and allow myself to enjoy this natural wonder. I sneak a glance at Fran and I know he's feeling this too. Something warm fills my chest and I realize what it is; I'm happy. I'm happy because I get to share this view with him.

'This is nothing,' he says, following the signs to the Grand Canyon National Park.

We pull up beside other cars, but we're the only people around. Like the only two humans on Mars.

'Turn around,' he says, holding on to my shoulders.

'Oh.'

It's such a small sound to make for what is spread out

before me. As far as the eye can see is red rock mixing with the blue haze of the afternoon. The ground drops beneath us and I stagger backwards.

'I'm not going any further,' I declare. I'm clutching Pushok to my chest and I must look freaking ridiculous holding a stuffed donkey over the precipice of the Grand Canyon.

'Just a little more,' Fran pleads. 'I promise it will be worth it.'

I move tentatively, because I don't like heights, and I'm getting images of the rock beneath us giving way and crumbling into the abyss below.

I cautiously peer down and my breath catches in my chest. I pant as I look out on the sheer beauty that is the Grand Canyon. I don't even know what to compare it to. The canyons are like golden craters from some alien desert in *Star Wars*. They dig into the earth, layered like some perfect pastry. A million shades of coral, sand, beige, gold and copper.

The hot wind whips my hair as I stare out over the horizon for what feels like hours but may only be a few minutes.

'Beautiful,' I say.

'Yeah,' Fran replies, but he's not looking at the view, he's looking at me. I turn but he looks away.

'All right,' I declare. 'I'm ready.' I take a step back towards the car.

'Oh no you don't,' says Fran, arms winding around my waist and pulling me back. 'We've got something else we need to do first.'

'Huh?'

He points his head in the direction of the canyon. 'Scream.'

'Excuse me?'

'Scream,' he repeats. 'It's on the list and you said you did it wrong. Scream into the void.'

The void. I stare out at the canyon. I'm annoyed that Fran keeps bringing it all back to the list. That it's so hard to enjoy this moment because it's all pulling me back to what I promised Lizzy.

I don't want to do what I'm told. I know he's just trying to help, to fix me or something, but I'm tired of him pushing.

I don't want to be helped, because I don't want to hope. I'm scared to believe everything will get better once I complete the list, and when it doesn't the pain will double.

'Maybe some other time,' I say. I take another step.

'Some other time when you are at the Grand Canyon?

That's not going to cut it, Nadejda. That's the voidiest void ever, and you're going to scream into it.'

I stiffen at the sound of my full name that he must have remembered from our earlier conversation. Then I turn and scowl at him.

'What are you going to do? Make me scream?'

Fran smiles. 'You wish.'

Anger explodes inside of me but also something fluttery.

'FINE!' I turn to the canyon and give a sharp scream.

Fran starts shaking his head.

'I need you to mean it.'

'You know what? You are the most infuriating, annoying . . .' I start but Fran doesn't listen, he just turns and walks away. I turn to the canyons instead and let loose a scream of frustration. Then another one. It actually feels pretty good. I scream louder. Pouring everything in my gut out into the canyons. When I'm done I turn around to find Fran staring at me.

'Damn,' he says. 'You got some pipes on you.'

'Your turn.'

'Huh?'

'You heard me, Francisco, your turn to scream. You think the whole world has something on their chest but you don't?'

Fran walks up to the edge.

He turns and screams. When it feels like he's screamed enough, I join him in a wolf howl.

We sit and eat Milk Duds and Charleston Chews, feet dangling off the precipice.

'I think Shawn will be happy to see you,' I say.

Fran shrugs, he doesn't look so sure.

'He has probably missed you as much as you've missed him.'

I'm not sure if that's true but I want to say something that makes Fran smile.

'How could he miss me?' says Fran, looking out over the horizon. 'What am I? Compared to all that he has now.'

His eyes don't shift from the canyon, and I can tell he's trying to make it sound a lot more casual than it's coming out. I nudge him.

'You're a person, Fran, not an object. The people we love are not replaceable.'

Then I put on my best Yoda accent.

'Unique you are. Replaceable you are not.'

I swear I hear him giggle.

CHAPTER 15

A poor man's Batman

I see the palm trees first. They look like the dusters that my mama buys at Poundland, feathery green tops pointing up at the sky. They hug the wide grey streets in tight formations. I gawk at them as we inch through traffic. I'm stuck to my window staring at everything like a child, like a dog with its tongue out the window lapping up the hot air. We roll slowly, inching across Hollywood Boulevard. I can't really believe it. *This is Los Angeles.* The LA from films and songs and shows.

The land of dreams.

I have to admit it doesn't really feel like the land of

195

dreams. There are tourists with large cameras weighing down their necks as they take whimsical photographs of the copper stars that mark the sidewalk. There are loads of tattoo parlours and neon-lit bong shops. There are a lot of pharmacy signs which I quickly realize are *dispensaries*. Places where you can get weed prescribed to you. There are people dressed in costumes on all the street corners, beckoning those same tourists. I see a poor man's Batman, an exceptional Charlie Chaplin, and a Marilyn Monroe; she's squatting seductively as if the steam is about to blow her white pleats up.

I yawn, and Fran's yawn follows instantly. After the canyons we spent the night at an off-road campsite to save time. The goal was to get here as quickly as possible, but now despite our excitement the lack of sleep is quickly catching up with us.

My heart clenches when I see the Chinese Theatre. I remember how Lizzy and I stayed up making Oscar predictions until 3 a.m. about films we weren't really intellectual enough to see. The only category we always knew well was special effects. But we made guesses with smart faces anyway and ate sugar-dusted hot cross buns. And there was something special about watching the celebs arrive in all their finery and glitz while icing sugar fell from my mouth on to the couch.

'WHO ARE YOU WEARING?' we'd wail dramatically. Until my brother would come in and yell at us to shut up.

It was the only night of the year that I convinced my parents to let Lizzy stay at our house. I told them that the Oscars gave us general knowledge that helped us on art history tests.

I blink and the Chinese Theatre is gone but the memory burns a little longer, a red ember.

'Are you okay?' I ask, distracting myself from the grief that's always so close to the surface.

'Yeah,' His eyes fixed on the car in front. 'So, let's eat something and then we will go to Shawn's house,' he says, as if grabbing a burger then visiting the home of one of the world's most famous people is something the two of us do regularly.

Fran's tense, his shoulders up around his ears. His leg is bouncing up and down so much it takes all my strength not to place my hand on it to calm him. I feel for him, but at the same time I'm so excited. I can't believe I'm going to finally meet Shawn Next, and he's going to write out Lizzy's name with a Sharpie, just like I've been imagining since the day his name was added to our list.

My body is fizzing and I don't know if my stomach is

aching from nerves, excitement or from how much I wish Lizzy were beside me right now.

'I think it's time you met Mexican food,' Fran says. 'The food of my people.'

'Hey, back home we have a burrito chain called Bandito Loco,' I say. 'I've been there a lot.'

Again there's Lizzy. She used to say *Life is short, always spring for the extra guac.*

'Yeah, Mexican food made by white English people is not Mexican food,' he says. 'Your mouth will burn,' he adds, and it reminds me of how much my mouth burned when he kissed me. 'And you'll love every second of it, that's *real* Mexican food,' he smiles. His tanned skin glows beautifully in the sun. I melt a little into the leather of my seat and look away.

Fran asks a few people on the street for recommendations in Spanish, and it leads us to a taco food truck with tables and chairs set out. We pick up our order and sit down.

Fran starts laying out dish after dish before me: burritos, tacos, salsa and little pots of dips. The colours are so bright, the scent of coriander and chilli so fresh. I take a bite and roll my eyes dramatically. Oh my God, he was right, *real* Mexican food made by Mexicans is glorious. I've nearly polished off my three fish tacos when something behind Fran freezes me into place.

A little lettuce falls from my mouth.

'That's attractive,' says Fran with a chuckle.

'Shut up,' I whisper. I stare at the lanky man ordering a taco, a beautiful woman by his side. I … *can't breathe.*

'That's Will Vogel!' I say.

'Who?'

'Shut up, don't look, shut up,' I squeal. And just like every other person in the universe who has ever been told to not look, Fran's head does a full 180.

'Oh my God, shut up, I said don't look,' I hiss.

'Who is that guy?'

'He's an actor who played a main character in a funny show Lizzy and I watched all the time when we were younger. *Green Oak Falls.*'

Fran watches him for a while.

'You're going to go and say hi,' he says, decidedly.

'Excuse me?'

'You're going to go up, and introduce yourself and thank him for the laughs,' says Fran as if it's the easiest thing to do in the world.

'No, I can't,' I stutter. Fran's dark eyes are intent on me.

I'm looking down trying to tune out the whole situation, when I feel Fran's fingers on my chin as he tilts my head back up to face him.

'Lizzy would want you to. This can be the thing that scares you. Since the ghost town didn't.' He winks at me.

It's a cheap shot and he knows it. He lets go, and I still feel where his fingers were on my face. He's right though.

A familiar pressure builds behind my eyes; it's true, Lizzy would have wanted me to do it. Courage somehow rises in me. I want to prove to Fran, and to Lizzy, and to myself, that I can do these things that paralyze me with fear. I rise and my knees are wobbly, threatening to give out under me. The tacos are threatening to reappear. I walk towards him. The girl with him looks like a supermodel and I think my legs have turned into actual jelly. I can't seem to walk properly.

I've watched this man since I was a kid. Watched him come in and out of episodes. Watched him make Lizzy snort-laugh. And here he is. He's been in my living room hundreds of times, but he doesn't know who I am. And that's a weird feeling.

I stalk up to him, looking like a strange disoriented goat. The model notices me first, Will Vogel second.

And the first phrase out of my mouth is . . .

'Hi there.' (I don't pause for him to answer.) 'So the

thing is, my best friend died last year . . .'

He moves back a little., 'Oh, um, okay.'

His okay is drawn out, like *oookaaay, what's that got to do with me?* He gives me that look like I'm about to ask for money. His companion looks nervous.

'I don't want anything from you.' I raise my hands in the air as if that's some kind of proof. 'I just need . . .' *Oh God, Nadia, shut your damn mouth and never open it again.* He's starting to back away. Slowly. As if I might attack. As if I'm one of those crazed fans that might try to slap him with my used tampon or fit him in the back of my car boot. The girl with him looks concerned too. I feel Fran materialize behind me. I'm too distracted to think about his hand on my hip, steadying me. I hate this whole interaction. I want the taco truck to run me over.

I breathe in deeply. Steady myself against the fear and the anxiety.

Fran's other hand lands on my shoulder. He gives me strength.

'What I was trying to say,' I start again, my voice more confident this time. 'I just needed to tell you, that my best friend and I watched *Green Oak Falls* for years. It was our favourite show and you were her favourite character. I wanted to say thank you for the laughs, and the memories and your work and … I watched it after she died and it helped me get through so thank you.'

I kind of plough through that whole bit like a school presentation. Without stopping to breathe. But I know I've done something right because his expression softens, so does the model's. She gives me a pearly-white smile.

'That means a lot,' he says. 'Thank you. And I'm really sorry about your friend.'

'It's okay.' I wave my hand in the air dismissively. What the hell am I doing? My face is sweating. 'I mean it's not *okay*, obviously. I just meant it's not your fault.' I let out a hysterical laugh. 'I mean HAHA HA why would it be your fault, that's just silly!' Will takes another step back, oh great.

'ANYWAY THANKS AND HAVE A NICE DAY?' *Why am I yelling at this poor man?*

'I think we will be going now,' says Fran. 'Thank you for your time.' His face is slightly contorted like he's trying really hard not to laugh. 'You both have a very nice rest of your day.'

I nod along vigorously. At this point I'm too star-struck to even say goodbye. Fran kind of leads me away, like I'm a disoriented grandma.

'Hope it gets better!' Will Vogel calls sweetly after us.

Oh God, God, God, could I have made any more of a fool of myself?

We turn the corner and I stop to calm down my shaking.

'I'm sorry,' says Fran, barely able to contain his laughter.

'It's not funny!'

'Look, you told him how much the show mattered to you and Lizzy, and that's really cool.'

'You sure?'

Fran looks serious now as he nods. 'You're a badass, Nadia.'

CHAPTER 16

Pain is an incoherent thing

We're sitting in Fran's Cadillac and I'm trying to still my heart. The PJs are scrunched in a ball growing more damp by the minute as the nerves get the better of me. If I don't calm down, I'll shove them violently right in Shawn Next's face and we will have a Will Vogel 2.0 scenario on our hands.

I'm about to meet Shawn Next. My insides squeal but I don't express it because I can see how tense Fran's entire body has gone. This is big for him as well, and for a fleeting moment I register that he's doing something that scares him too.

I look up and take in the building beside us. We are sitting outside the fanciest house I've ever seen. Fancier than anything I saw when I went with Dad to pick up deliveries sometimes. This place is like something straight out of *Selling Sunset*. I imagine Shawn opening the door and leading us in, showing us his transparent fridge full of coconut water and Moët champagne. Maybe he'll take us to his indoor skateboarding ring and show us a few 360s or whatever they're called. I'm lost in my fantasy of the outrageous home interiors of the rich and famous, flinching as Fran waves a hand in front of me.

'Earth to Nadiaaaaa,' he says in a mock Russian accent. I flash him a scathing look and he gives me a lopsided smile.

'You ready?'

'Yeah.' I unclench my fist and release the pyjamas, after nearly having given myself carpal tunnel from how tightly I was clutching them. There are now wet spots of sweat on the fabric. I feel like I'm underwater, like I'm watching myself in a movie, like my soul is ten feet above my body. I'm so out of it I don't even realize that Fran is opening the car door for me.

We've parked on a wide street surrounded by houses that look like they were built by architects trying to show off. Fran's beloved car is the only vehicle on the empty street. I guess rich people park their cars in garages or have chauffeur-driven limos that pick them up.

We walk up a winding driveway till we hit the house, a large minimalist structure that looks like it cost millions. Fran stares at it with a distrusting expression, and I notice the slightest tremor in his hands. I would reach for him if my own hands weren't frozen claws clutched around my pyjamas.

I think of Lizzy, visualizing her face so intensely I almost think I can reach out and touch her. This is all for her. It's what she wanted. It's Lizzy's moment as much as it is mine. Her last wish.

Beside me Fran steadies himself, and almost imperceptibly rights his shirt.

He rings the doorbell and everything in me freezes. This is it.

Nothing.

Fran looks at me. He rings it again. I hear distant footsteps. A man opens the door, a man with tired eyes and three-day-old stubble. Definitely not Shawn Next. He looks at us, first at Fran, then at me, then at Fran again. His eyes linger a little longer on Fran, suspicious.

'Yeah?' He says it like a question.

'We're looking for Shawn,' says Fran.

The man rubs his eyes like we just asked the world's most exhausting question.

'What?'

Someone is yelling after him in the house and he looks behind him, distracted. A baby cries.

'Who is it, Jack?' screams a woman from a room that seems impossibly far away.

'One second, Irene,' he yells back irritably. 'Jesus what do we even have two nannies for?' he mumbles under his breath before turning back to us, still confused.

'Shawn Next,' I say. My voice is weaker than I'd like and my words come out more like a plea than I want them to.

His eyes travel to my hand and they linger on the pyjamas and the Sharpie I bought at a 7-Eleven.

With a heavy sigh he tries to slam the door in our face but Fran is quicker.

'No,' Fran says simply, as he plants his foot in the door. 'We need to talk to him. It's important. He knows me.'

'Get the hell out of my doorway or I'll call the police,' the man says. Fran takes a tiny step back, like a boy who has been threatened by cops before.

207

'We bought this house from him like two years ago and you people keep coming,' says Jack. 'You weirdos.'

'Screw you,' says Fran.

'Do you have a forwarding address?' I say from behind Fran. 'Please, anything. It's really important.'

'No and even if I did I wouldn't give it to you,' he says. 'Crazy-ass stalker fans,' he mumbles but it's loud enough for us to hear. He slams the door in our face.

Fran kicks it in anger.

Defeated, I walk off, silently getting back in the car. As we drive away, Fran says something about us renting a place in Venice Beach for the night. I don't even really hear him. I just watch the streets, dog walkers walking by us like the world hasn't just ended, as if this whole trip hasn't been for nothing. Disappointment burns through me so strongly that my eyes start to fill up with tears of shame and frustration. Everything.

I was a fool. I am a fool.

I'm never getting our PJs signed. I'm never going to finish Lizzy's list. I'm as much of a disappointment to her in death as I was in life. I'm nothing.

We reach Venice quickly. Fran parks next to signs that point at a strip.

'Come here.' Fran reaches for me, like he wants to hug me, but I push him away.

The idea of being touched repulses me. The anger runs too deep. I want to destroy things, for the world outside to reflect how I feel.

I push his hands away. He blinks. The hollowness inside me expands. It bubbles, mounts and trips over itself. Lava rising from a volcano.

I'm nothing. She's never coming back. I'm nothing.

I am nothing without her. The pain is an incoherent thing. It swirls and I can't put it into words except that it's unbearable. I get out of the car. Fran follows me. I need air. I can't breathe.

'I'm never getting her back. It's over.' The phrase out loud seems ridiculous. Of course I'm never getting her back, she's dead for Christ's sake.

He reaches for me again. 'I know how you feel,' he whispers.

'No, no you don't know,' I snap back.

My tears are fat, hot globs making their way down my face freely. Rage is a mean black fire in me, but it's better than the hollowness. I want to burn. It erupts and I spew fire. I walk down the street. Away from Fran, blindly towards the strip, towards the beach. I want to be alone. I want to die.

He catches up to me. 'Wait up, Nadia, I'm upset too you know. Could you stop to think about how scared I've been, driving to see the friend who abandoned me. You made me believe I could finish something too, and now it's all messed up. So, yeah I *do* know how you feel.'

He knows how I feel? Why does he keep saying that?

The air is taut between us. Fran reaches out and strokes my cheek, cupping it. He closes the remaining distance between us till his forehead is nearly touching mine. I'm aware that if I tilt my head up and move an inch I would be kissing him again. Maybe for real this time. I could drown in him, the touch of his hands, the feel of his lips on mine, and forget everything.

But the trouble is I can't forget. Anger and pain floods my veins and stays there, pulsating beneath the skin.

'You don't know how I feel,' I say venomously. 'Someone leaving you because they became famous is not the same. He *chose* to leave you. They ... the people who hurt you, they made choices but at least they are still alive. Lizzy didn't want to leave me. She wanted to stay, she ... she didn't get a choice.' My voice cracks. Fran takes a shocked step back.

I can see the virtual slap on Fran's face and I didn't even lift a finger. But his skin is reddening with blotches where my fingers would have struck. His beautiful brown face is paling, his lips pursing slightly.

'*They chose to* …' Fran repeats after me, staring blankly at the beach. 'I never thought of it that way, Nadia,' he says. I want to reach for him but I don't.

Because on top of my guilt and my aching heart I have a layer of rage and pride and venom, thick like scar tissue.

'You're right,' he says, as if he's still contemplating it. Then he walks past me, light on his feet. And away down the Venice strip. People swallow him. He's gone.

I let him go.

CHAPTER 17

A type of cracker that fixes everything

Fran has no idea what he's talking about. No idea what it's like to watch your best friend deteriorate and disappear. He thinks we've lived through the same pain and we haven't. I fume as I roam the Venice streets. I know I'm looking for trouble. It's this darkness inside me stirring, it's waking up and it's hungry, and I'm going to feed it. People wash over and past me as I search for something. Eyes scanning the grimy strip.

It's past dinner time but I'm not hungry. A bass thumps down the street, vibrating the dirty pavement. I walk past marijuana-shaped key chains, tattoo shops that buzz like beehives, and racks of polyester underwear. I find the source of the bass.

I can't believe my luck as I descend the tight, dank stairway that leads into a nightclub below ground. They didn't even card me! I enter a room with low ceilings and a ball of hot air hits me in the face. The smell of sweat and cologne with the lightest undertone of urine.

I walk straight to the bar as if I belong there. A man next to it looks up. He's smartly dressed and in his late twenties, maybe older. He looks like he has money, like the whiskey he's drinking is the most expensive in this club and he's not used to hearing *no*.

His eyes give me the once-over, his thin mouth curling as if he likes what he sees and he normally gets what he wants. I should be afraid. I'm alone, six thousand miles from my family. In a dimly lit club in Los Angeles, with nowhere to sleep and no one to call, and nothing to call them with. Because my phone is still in the car. I don't care though. Because nothing is worse than what's already happened. That's what I tell myself and order a shot, knocking it back in one mouthful. The man by the bar watches me with amusement. I cringe against the roughness of the alcohol.

Not enough.

I take another shot and begin to dance.

My body moves on its own. My eyes are half closed, lids heavy. I want to lose myself, to become nothing. My fingers sink into the shadows of the dance floor.

I'm so close to feeling like a part of the darkness instead of a victim to it. I jump on my heels to the music and I'm vaguely aware of bodies pushing up against me. Of wet skin sliding on wet skin. I stop only to stumble back to the bar. The barman gives me a brief look, but it's not really his job to judge. I'm out of money. I dig for quarters in the back pocket of my jeans, littering the bar with them. The room is hazy but I want it to blur more, and then I want it to disappear completely. Someone hands me a drink.

It's the man who was checking me out earlier.

He's wearing a blazer and a button-down, even though he's on a night out. As if he came here straight from the office. He's clean-shaven and his features are angular.

I chug the drink. He smiles at me. His teeth are so white. I nod as he hands me another shot. We down them. I grimace and he laughs, as if I'm endearing.

'You're cute,' he yells over the music, like I'm some stuffed animal at a gas station. My stomach tightens as I think of Pushok. Thoughts of Fran, where he is, if he's looking for me, push past my drunken haze. Then Lizzy, but I can't go there. I throw my largest wall up, black marble, to keep the thoughts away. I tug at the banker's tie, smiling up at him. He buys me another drink.

'My name is Steve,' he says. I hate his name the instant it hits my ears, but I smile as if I don't.

'My name is Nadia,' I yell over the music. His eyes narrow.

'Where are you from?' That dreaded question.

The truth threatens to pour out of me.

I'm from nowhere. I'm lost. I'm nothing.

'I'm English.'

He smirks. 'English?' Then he leans seductively towards me. His tequila breath stings my eyes. 'Are you a Bond girl?'

I can tell he thinks he's made the most original of jokes.

I don't tell him that I think that's the lamest line I've ever heard.

But I want more alcohol, and I don't care that his chat is weak.

I tilt my face up to meet his. I bat my eyelashes.

'If I told you I'd have to kill you,' I tell him in my best impression of Aunt Larissa's flirtatious tone.

'Oh no, I'm not going to try and make you angry then ... or maybe I should?' He smiles seductively.

Steve smells like expensive aftershave.

I don't even know what he's saying to be honest. He's stringing words together, like strands of sugar, and it's supposed to be a sweet compliment, but when I reach for it, it crumbles.

Fran's words never sound like that.

Nausea threatens my vision. 'I'm going for a walk on the beach.'

Steve tries to grab my hand but I wave him off and run up the stairs. The coat check flashes before my eyes, then the stairway, then the security guard's face. Suddenly everything speeds up again like in a music video. I'm back on the strip of Venice Beach. There are thick swarms of people. I squint against the neon lighting of the souvenir shops.

I plant my feet to the ground and double over. Steve materializes behind me. I wish he'd go away.

I'm going to throw up. One hundred per cent.

Steve waits for a while then he says, 'Are you going to puke?'

Go away, I want to say, but acid fills my mouth. The pre-vomit acid, that lets you know you should stay

216

doubled over. That staying low to the ground is your safest bet.

Steve tries to straighten me out as if he can just force my nausea away. I straighten a tiny bit, trying to push his hands away. I don't want him here, I don't want him touching me.

Through half-hooded eyes I glare at him. Then I swing my knee up, right into his balls.

He howls.

'What the—?' He swings as if to backhand me. But a fist connects with his face instead. Fran stands firmly between us.

Steve stumbles to a standing position. Hand on his jaw. He takes Fran in, the anger clearly etched on his face, clenched fists at his sides. I can see Steve weighing his options, deciding whether it's worth fighting Fran. By the look on Fran's face I doubt he would win.

'Move, *pendejo*,' Fran growls.

'I could take you,' Steve mutters but he skitters away nonetheless.

I turn to Fran. I stumble, 'I don't need your protection! I was handling it! I don't need you to come on your white horse and save me. I don't . . . I don't!' I'm vaguely aware of being incoherent. But I don't need help. That's the point. I don't need help because I just want everything to stop. And I don't need his help for that. I can do it all on my own.

'Nadia.' My name on his lips pushes me over the edge. I stagger away from him. My rage gives way to pain, pain so deep I'm sinking in it. I'm ashamed Fran saw me like this, with that horrible man.

He calls after me as I sprint, not down the strip but towards the beach. My feet sink into the sand. I'm running, running, running, until the sand grows hard and wet and I plunge my body into the foamy cold ocean.

I'm knee-deep; I go further. When I feel the bite of cold water at my waist, I dive head first. The water is freezing and black. I hold my breath under its weight.

Suddenly I'm wide awake and conscious of the burn in my throat. I want air. I want it more than I've ever wanted anything and suddenly I'm terrified. I pull up and Fran is a few paces away. He grabs hold of me.

'Nadia! Nadia!' He shakes with disbelief, as if he's unsure whether it's me or a jellyfish he just caught.

I fumble for him, bunching his wet shirt in my hands, and I pull and press against him. A groan bubbles out of me. Relief and shame and drunkenness. I'm still greedily gulping air when the gulps turn into sobs. He flattens his hand against my wet back and strokes, rhythmically, pulling me closer to him. A wave hits us sideways but he holds strong against it. Keeping me still.

He kisses my wet hair.

'You scared me, Nadejda.' He says my full name. He says it correctly. His eyes glisten in the moonlight as if he too is about to cry. He truly looks scared.

I want to pull him down. To say sorry. To press my face into his neck.

Fran's eyes settle on mine as he closes any distance left between us. He brushes his thumb under my eye, in a soft dragging motion. To wipe away the tears even though we are both soaked. Then kisses my forehead. And I feel like my heart might explode out of my chest. His touch feels like an electric current. I want to kiss him so badly.

Instead I turn and vomit in the sea.

Fran helps me out of the waves.

He supports me and we walk through the steep alleyways that lead away from Venice Beach. Cats slink behind bins, back from their midnight meet ups, and I see small black roaches scattering too, with that nasty crackling sound that they make. I push the rest of the vomit down. The chilly salty air is sobering; the wetness of my clothes makes me shiver. We stop by an all-night drugstore and Fran instructs me to wait. I lean against one of those traffic light buttons, and press it, listening to it click in response just so that I can occupy myself with something. Partygoers don't pay me any attention. I can smell weed wafting around, but it's not coming from the dispensary on the corner, where a neon sign blinks on and off announcing KUSH DOCTORS HERE. I inhale more salty air, deep gulps, sending them up into my brain to clear my head. Fran hurries back out, flimsy white bag in hand. He hands me a cold ginger ale.

'I got you some Alka-Seltzer, and saltines,' he says a little awkwardly. He looks guilty, though I don't know what he has to feel guilty about, I'm the jerk here.

He wraps me in a beach towel with a dolphin on it.

'What are saltines?' I ask.

'A type of cracker that fixes everything.'

His brown eyes are sad. I don't want him to feel guilty. It's not his fault I drank so much. Not his fault I met that man or ran into the sea. None of this is his fault. Not his fault we are both here. He brought me here to help me and I was too selfish to see that he needed help too. I can't bring myself to say anything though because I'm still not one hundred per cent certain that vomit won't come out instead of words. I gargle with some ice-cold water he bought for me, then drink the ginger ale. I eat the saltines, which I have to admit are a little divine. We sit there on the kerb for what feels like ages, until the shivering stops.

He walks me a few blocks further and down a side street until we hit a huge development, with one of those puckered textured surfaces that makes it look like the building is made from a mix of cement and gravel. He produces a key from his back pocket and he opens the door. I gawk.

'Who lives here?' I ask as he leads me to the grey lift.

'I got us an Airbnb,' he said. He shrugs his shoulders, and looks hesitant. He's speaking very gently, like I'm a wild animal he lured in with some ham, like I will scare from loud words or quick movements. He pushes his wet hair back and presses number *four*.

We ride the lift in silence, except for the drip coming off the edge of my clothes. I pull the dolphin towel tighter around myself. I look at Fran but I look away when he turns.

The lift opens and we walk down an open-air hallway that allows you to see the small courtyard below. He slides a key into the lock of a door at the end of the hall and it gives way. I cross the apartment's hallway and go into the living room.

'It's not great, but the hotels were a fortune and I ... was worried I wouldn't find you ... so I didn't want to go far. I booked this then walked up and down the strip looking for you and ...' Fran's unfinished sentence hangs in the air like a summer garland, sparkling in the night-time. I wander around the apartment. There's a breakfast bar, a kitchen that looks a little worn for wear, and a bedroom with nothing but a bed. Low to the ground. I go to the rectangle window, framed by flimsy blinds that look like shredded paper. I look out.

LA is some kind of rare breed of shitty beauty. I look out at the low yet sprawling city. It's no New York with its grandeur. It's no London with its welcoming river and rich history.

It's something in-between, as if someone built a ghetto in a beautiful place, then threw some mansions and palm trees in the mix for good measure. I turn and find Fran in the doorway. Cautious, alert, afraid. I've never seen him like this.

'I scared you,' I say. He nods.

'I'm just happy you're safe.' His wet hair catches the

222

light. One stubborn curly strand escapes the rest and falls over his forehead.

'I bought you some hair dye.' He gestures at two boxes in the kitchen. 'Wasn't sure what colour you would want so I got blue and pink, but we can change them. If you want. I have the receipt.'

He's rambling. I'm quiet, amazed by him. Even in his anger he remembers the list.

Number 10 – Dye your hair a wild colour.

I was so horrible to him.

'Anyway. I'll let you sleep, I'll take the couch.' He nods his chin towards the living room.

'Wait.' My voice is a croak as I walk up to him. I kiss him, quick and feather-light. Just a swift brush of my lips on his and yet it feels like lightning. Fran stares at me but I can't read his expression.

My fingers shake as I unbutton my wet blouse and peel it back like a layer. Standing there in my damp bra, I'm suddenly conscious of my small bra size.

Fran looks like a boy who is trying to pretend he doesn't want to look.

I move my fingers to my jeans, but he swoops his hands out and stills mine.

I've misread the signs and I blush deeply. I'm an idiot.

Why would he want me? After everything he's seen? After everything I've said? And if all of that wasn't enough tonight would have pushed him away for good. Christ, I vomited in the ocean in front of him! I take a step back, embarrassed.

'It's not . . .' he says, and again the sentence just hangs there.

He reaches for my hips and tugs me closer. I look up and find longing in his eyes and it helps some of my evaporated confidence return. He takes a step towards me. His lips are against my hair. If I reached I could kiss him.

'It's not that I don't want to. I do,' he whispers.

'So, what's the problem?'

I know what he's going to say. I look terrible, I reek of seawater. I'm a total mess and a screw-up. Why would he want me?

He leans closer. His lips hovering above my ear now, my bra touching his damp T-shirt.

'You're drunk, upset. When it happens, I don't want it to be like this. I don't want to be someone you regret in the morning.'

I look at him. I want to tell him there's nothing about him that I could ever regret. But I know that face. He's resolute. There's no point arguing.

'Can we sleep together? Just sleep.'

Fran smiles. 'Sure.'

We climb into bed and I settle my head on his chest, close to his heartbeat.

Eventually we fall asleep. Our salty, damp, warm bodies wrapped around each other like a pretzel.

A tangle of parts and limbs that fit perfectly.

I don't have any nightmares. Instead, I dream of the sea.

CHAPTER 18

The biggest pancake breakfast you have ever seen

Waking in the morning, I reach for Fran but find the bed empty. A sudden panic seizes me as I rise and go to the empty living room. Is he gone? Did I push him too far?

I don't want to be someone you regret in the morning.

What if he regrets *me*? The girl that showed up and got him fired and into two fights. The girl that can't stop crying. The girl that launched herself into the sea.

I find our luggage in the living room and brush my teeth. I ignore my dead phone. Relief floods through me when I hear a jangle of keys and Fran enters the room, carrying two coffees.

'Good morning,' he says, handing me one.

I take a heavenly sip and then set it down. 'It is a good *morning*, isn't it?' I smile wide, emphasizing the word. I laugh.

'What's so funny?' His thick brows bunch up. He takes a slow sip of his coffee and leans against the breakfast bar, so relaxed, like this is our routine every day. I just keep smiling, unnerving him. Cautiously, he smiles back.

I step closer until we're toe to toe and he's towering over me. His long black lashes are stark against his tanned face. He cocks a brow.

'What are you scheming, Nadejda? You're making me nervous.'

I reach up. I'm on my tiptoes, and kiss his Adam's apple.

For a fleeting moment his brow furrows, his eyes full of questions.

'You can't regret someone in the morning, if it's already morning,' I tell him. He sighs with a small smile, his eyes blinking slowly, nose rubbing against mine as he looks down. He stalls, our heartbeats knocking against one another, his lips stealing my breaths, and then he kisses me. His touch is gentle, like the brush of a feather upon my skin, hesitant but inquisitive. I pull away.

'I want this,' I say, ensuring he fully understands that this isn't because of last night, and this isn't another thing to tick off the list or something. This is real. 'I want you, *Fran*.'

My voice breaks on his name and he comes undone.

This time Fran doesn't hesitate, our mouths collide, his kiss gets deeper, stronger, than that first kiss in the ghost town. With one hand he pulls me to him by the waist, his other hand lost in my hair. His kiss is a scorching desert, my lips burning, my skin on fire. He tastes like salt. Then his hands are cupping my face, stroking my cheekbones with his thumbs, holding me like I'm something unbreakable, not something broken.

Everything colliding at once. My Gosling kiss.

I pull him after me, through the living room and on to the bed. His kisses grow harder, more urgent, his mouth travelling across my lips, down my jaw and to my neck.

I pull off his T-shirt and throw it aside. He meets my mouth again, like he never wants to break our connection. He helps me pull my jeans off, with each movement checking it's okay. I do the same for him, his mouth never leaving mine.

He stops suddenly, and I falter, my need for him like a gnawing ache.

'Have you done this before?' he asks in one rush of air, the two of us out of breath, his eyes never leaving mine. I nod slightly.

'Only a couple of times.'

I'm terrified my admission will make him change his mind, or maybe it will put him at ease. His expression shifts a little.

'Same,' he says. Then he kisses me again and we melt into one another, his warm chest against mine.

'Nadia.' His eyes are bright, the sunlight from the window reflecting in them, bringing out the honey tones in the brown.

'Are you absolutely sure that you want this?' he whispers against my ear.

I nod again. I've been so alone, blocking everyone out for months. But being here with Fran is different, and what we are about to do feels right. *Everything* with Fran feels right.

'Yes,' I say against the dryness of my throat. He smiles a little sheepishly and his mouth is on mine again.

Fran is gentle and slow and we move as one for eternity, our lips and eyes never leaving one another, until we are both spent – a tangle of sweaty limbs and panting breaths.

He flips to his back and turns to nuzzle in my neck.

'Are you all right?' he whispers.

I do a quick assessment: legs are wobbly, cheeks flushed, my head is pounding and my breaths irregular. I don't feel sad, which is weird because I'm so used to always feeling sad that the absence of it is like a lightness. Like swimming.

'I'm fine, I'm good,' I say.

It takes me a minute to process the fact that there's a very sexy, tattooed, naked boy in my bed, with the sheets wrapped around his midsection, the way you would see in a film. And then my stomach grumbles and ruins it all.

'I'm going to take you to the biggest pancake breakfast you have ever seen,' he says, stroking a piece of hair from my forehead. 'Think pools of maple syrup, think waffles, think hash browns and ketchup, and a stack of pancakes that looks like a small house.'

The hungover part of me feels an intense hunger stir in my stomach.

'That sounds like heaven,' I say. 'But first,' I grapple again.

And he grapples back.

*

I stare over my mountain of pancakes at Fran. His eyes are golden in the diner sunshine. God he's handsome.

I gesture around. 'Back to your roots.'

We met in a diner. Things have come full circle.

He nods and smiles, but he's busy stuffing his face with triangular hash browns. Do boys get super hungry after sex?

I've learned that, much like death, sex makes you want to google the crap out of everything. I resist the urge to google whether or not the fact that I've made Fran ravenous is a good thing.

'I have a surprise for you,' he says, wiping his mouth with a napkin. He grins and it fills my heart to the brim. I've never seen him smile quite like this.

He reaches into his bag and pulls out some papers and two cards. He pushes all of it across the chrome table towards me.

I stare at the laminated cards and two slips of paper, dumbstruck.

'OH MY GOD,' I gasp, and then I squeal. A few people in the diner turn to stare at me. 'But how did you ... did you track him down?' My head is swirling with questions. Did Fran go and find Shawn Next while I was dancing in Venice? While I was asleep this morning? I'm holding two tickets to tonight's concert and two laminated backstage passes.

Fran doesn't answer and digs back into his food.

'Fran, where did you get these?'

'I bought them,' he says after a beat.

Bought them? I'm holding like three thousand dollars' worth of tickets. Where the hell would he get that kind of money?

My eyes drift to the parking lot by our window. Oh. No. *No no no no.*

'You sold your car?' It's not really a question, I know he did. We walked from the Boulevard last night. We walked to the diner this morning. I haven't seen his car since yesterday. He sold his beloved Cadillac, cherry red. Just to buy concert tickets.

'How? When?'

'Went to one of those *we buy any car now with cash* places. Got the tickets at a vendor on Venice Beach. Then walked around the Boulevard to look for you.'

He keeps eating. I can't even reach for my food. The guilt and gratitude are a deadly concoction inside of me.

'But Fran, you love that car. I didn't want you to, I never meant for you to . . .'

To sell something you love.

'And you need it for work, and it's your only income source, we have to go get it back!'

My head is flooded with images of Fran eating ramen for the rest of his life. He reaches out and grasps my hand, which is still clutching my fork stupidly.

'It's okay, I still have my dad's old Prius, and it's way better for the environment anyway.' He waves his hand in what I know is false dismissal. 'But *this* . . . mission we are on. We are finishing it.'

CHAPTER 19

Beans and Things

'What are we doing here?'

I look up at the coffee shop called *Beans and Things*. Looking up at places and asking Fran what the hell we are doing there is beginning to become a serious déjà vu. I like that he's into surprises though . . .

After our breakfast of kings he made a big deal of leading me here, refusing to tell me where he was taking me. Not that I would ever admit I'd follow him anywhere.

'It's a pit stop before we get ready for the concert.'

I groan. 'I'm already over-caffeinated, and overfed.'

'We are not here to eat or drink.' Fran pushes through the door and holds it open for me.

'I know the mysterious and brooding thing is part of your charm, but you need to tone it down,' I joke as I go inside. The moment my eyes settle on the interior of the café my feet suddenly feel glued to the floor.

'*No,*' I say.

'Yes.'

'No. Absolutely not.'

Fran tugs me deeper into the wood-panelled interior. There are lots of plants, driftwood bits and vines, iced lattes in mason jars and a barista that wears a silk headscarf tied in a bow and looks awfully cool. Fran probably hates this kind of place, the kind of place that just screams hipster on a typewriter. But it's not the decor that makes me stall, it's the tiny stage in the corner of the room, and the microphone there on its skinny black stand. I try to resist but Fran kisses the back of my hand, which makes me thaw a little, and before I know it we are sat down at a table made of upcycled pallets.

'They have open mic poetry readings at lunchtime,' he says.

Of course they do.

'Yeah, I gathered that,' I answer solemnly.

235

'You can do this, Nadia.'

Fran's belief in me is like a hot air balloon – it lifts me up but it's also terrifying to go near.

I'm still grumbling when he fetches us two coffees.

'I put your name on the list,' he says, as he examines his mason jar sceptically.

A few minutes later the scarf-clad barista taps the microphone and starts to call out names.

I always thought that open mics at cafés featured people aggressively reading out spoken-word pieces about the government or erotically charged poems about the ocean, but to my great dismay the first few people to go before me are good. Like, *really good.* I sink further into my seat.

'Do you know what you will read?' Fran whispers.

I reach into my bag and pull out the journal Larissa gave me. I've scribbled a few poems in it during my trip.

Shit. Shit. Shit. I can't do this. I try to breathe.

I'm contemplating making a dash for it, but that seems too dramatic. Or maybe I could go up there and read someone's else's poem. Like a famous person's poem. Will anyone even be able to tell if I spit out some Lord Byron? This is LA. They probably think Lord Byron is someone Prince Harry plays polo with.

But I don't know any Lord Byron poems by heart.

The barista calls my name, and with shaking hands I scowl playfully at Fran and get up onstage.

My voice comes out stale when I speak. 'Hi, my name is Nadejda and I'm from London.'

Do they need my last name?

Some idiot yells something about the Royal Family and Fran shoots him a death glare. A woman at the front gives me this super cheesy encouraging look. I get closer to the microphone.

'My poem is called "I Try".' It's too late, I'm falling off the cliff and I might as well embrace the fall. I tune the room out and focus on the journal, even though the hand holding it is shaking. I find Fran's eyes. Hold his gaze, breathe and dive in.

'I think of you in the mornings
I think of you in the evenings . . .

I think of you, in the middle of the night,
Nightmares about that call, keep me awake
When I recall, crying your name
And how badly,
I wanted you to stay,

But your final call, so loud,
Put all my other calls to shame

But now I try . . .

To think of you each day
Remembering the way
The way you were, not now
But then,
How you danced, and sang and frowned
And laughed so loud
And wanted ice cream every day

I smile, remembering those days
Not now, not at the end,
Not at the call
But how you were, inside my head,
Tucked in my heart, etched in my soul
Before it all, before it all.'

I stop and it feels like the world has stopped with me, one second stretching into hours. Do I walk away or bow or say thank you?

I take a deep breath and just wait, realizing I hardly

breathed through that whole thing. Someone claps and it startles me. Then more people clap and I see Fran beaming from the back, giving me a standing ovation.

With tears in my eyes and my heart thundering in my ears I scramble off the stage and hurry over to him. People are still clapping. Then the barista announces the next name and it's all over. I try to calm my body and stop it from shaking, but no amount of deep breaths are going to get my adrenaline levels back to normal. Fran and I stay through the next two readers out of politeness, then I grab his hand and we jet out.

The warm outside air hits me, calming me, the surge of fear and excitement more of a simmering fizz now.

'That was insane!' I say, grinning at him. I feel proud of myself.

'You were amazing,' Fran says. He kisses me and I let his kiss take me whole.

'I'm done being this vulnerable by the way,' I say once we pull apart. 'You're going to need to show me your darkest deepest secrets too!'

'I don't have any.' Fran's hair looks almost light brown in the white sun.

'I'm serious, you've seen me throw up,' I say.

'Twice,' he corrects with a smile. Then he kisses me again.

'Fine. Twice,' I say, kissing him back. 'AND you know my dark secrets, and now you've heard my poetry and seen me drunk. I demand payment for such vulnerability. I demand one honest answer.'

Fran's mouth is on mine again, teasing me. I shove him playfully.

'Stop trying to change the subject.'

'Fine. Ask me whatever you want. I'll give you one honest answer.'

'What do you want to be when you grow up? What's your big dream?'

He contemplates this. 'At NYU, I want to study documentary filmmaking,' he says, surprising me yet again.

CHAPTER 20

The Next big thing

The stadium is far bigger than I imagined, and weirdly named after an office supply store chain.

If only Lizzy could see me now. I'm hand in hand with a sexy guy, in LA, in front of the Staples Center, with backstage passes to the Shawn Next concert. I allow myself a moment to recall her giddy face, the one she got if her crush winked at her, or on Christmas mornings when she FaceTimed me to show off her new Topshop clothes, or when the latest K-pop video she had been waiting for finally released.

I give myself just one more second to remember. Just

a taste of sweetness before it normally turns to bitterness on my tongue. But I won't let the sadness come, not tonight. When I think of Lizzy, joy and sadness seem intertwined like roots, impossible to untangle. But my poem reminded me that I can focus on the joy alone, home in on it – remembering the beauty of *then* without the ugliness of *after*.

I grin up at Fran. He's wearing a faded T-shirt and a jean jacket that looks gorgeous on him. He insisted on buying an outfit for us both.

Though Fran looks amazing, he looks nervous too. His tattooed arms are exposed beneath rolled up sleeves, and he keeps readjusting them. I'm wearing a sparkly green dress, with beads sewn on. My new blue hair is curly and wild over my shoulders.

We pass the fans in the regular line. I feel a little bit of embarrassment in front of Fran as I look out on their flushed faces. The young girls wearing Shawn Next tees, and home-made headbands, and poster-board signs that say things like *Please let me be Next*, and *Shawn, you are our heart*. I decide not to tell Fran about the time Lizzy and I dressed up as versions of Shawn Next songs to go see his concert film at its midnight release. But then I tell myself there's nothing to be embarrassed about, fandom can sometimes be the sole reason people choose to keep going.

Despite his nervousness Fran looks excited too. I squeeze his hand.

We are so close to the stage, almost touching it, sandwiched by other fans. I look around the stadium and it's cavernous inside, dotted with thousands of lightsabers. *Hey, I made a* Star Wars *reference!* Look at me. Lizzy would be proud. After a quick opening act by a rising country starlet, the concert begins in earnest, and Shawn Next swoops on to the stage amid an array of impressive pyrotechnics. I look at Fran. He seems a little taken aback to be seeing his childhood best friend in the flesh and onstage in front of thousands of people. But he adapts quickly once the music starts and we begin dancing.

I listen to the familiar songs, soaking them in. I close my eyes and I let memories of Lizzy and these songs wash over me: of pyjamas and stolen gin, nicked from her mum's drinks cabinet; of Korean sheet masks with zebra faces on them; of manicures that looked like they were done by glitter-crazed three-year-olds. When I close my eyes, I see a photo montage of mine and Lizzy's friendship.

I start to cry when Shawn Next sings 'A Time for Us', one of his few slow ballads. And I cry through some of his sadder new songs. Ones I haven't listened to properly yet.

Fran hugs me from behind. He knows why I'm crying. Not because I'm some super-fan melting before Shawn's co-ordinated dance moves, but because *this* is Lizzy. She's somehow not gone; memories of her fill me and they don't make me hollow or sad. I'm full of gratitude to have them, floating like sparkling snowflakes in the orbit of my mind.

Fran winds his arms tighter around me, and we dance till our feet hurt.

When the concert ends we head to the VIP section to get backstage access. A security guard checks our passes and lets us through. Backstage there is a buffet and a few other wide-eyed fans with passes. My gaze is briefly drawn to the free champagne.

But there's no Shawn anywhere.

Fran and I head over to a second guard.

'Where is Shawn?' Fran calls over the stadium's loud music.

'He's about to leave,' says the guard.

What?!

'He's not coming out?' I gasp.

'He was already out here briefly, these celebs never stay backstage for long,' the guard explains, waving his hand dismissively.

Fran turns and looks at me.

I think he can see disappointment spreading through me but I squash it down. Fran has given me so much, I can't let him down. I can see that now.

'Fran, it doesn't matter. This was one of the best nights of my life, I already feel like I won, I don't need the PJs signed,' I tell him. 'You've given me so much more.' He starts to shake his head.

'No, screw that, we are finishing this.' He eyes the burly guard to his left. Then looks back at me. 'Follow my lead.'

Oh, no.

Fran holds my hand gingerly as he leads me to another guard positioned at the second backstage entrance. Fran gets very close to him on one side. The guard hasn't noticed us yet. And at the last possible moment Fran yells, 'RUN!'

I jet after him and past the guard. I hear the guard

bellow after us as he breaks into a sprint. We are running as fast as we can, past a maze of equipment and doors. My legs shake in protest, but I propel myself forward, keeping close to Fran, even though he set a fast pace.

We turn into unknown hallways, run past surprised staff. The guard's shouts follow us as our feet pound along the corridors.

Just when I feel like I can't run any more, my chest fit to burst, we spot Shawn Next and his entourage walking down a hall a few feet away. Fran pulls me forward but it's too late.

The guards are upon us. There are at least three of them.

One grabs my hand and yanks me back. I scream. They drag me backwards.

'S-DAWG!' Fran calls and Shawn's head whips around. He stops and stares at us. Then he keeps walking. Did he not hear him?

The guards are pulling us back, dragging us down the hall away from him, the heels of our trainers squeaking along the floor.

'S-DAWG!' Fran calls out again, louder this time.

Really? S-Dawg?

Shawn Next turns again, and breaks from his

entourage. He walks the length of the hall and stops before us.

'Franny?' he says disbelievingly. 'What the hell?'

'They snuck past us, sir,' says the guard. Shawn waves his hand at him dismissively.

'It's cool, they're with me. Let them go.'

The guard releases me and they all back away silently, standing nearby just in case.

I can't believe I'm looking right at Shawn Next. My jaw drops a little. *And he calls him Franny! That's why Fran hated it.* Shawn is even more handsome in person. Sparkling blue eyes, gravity-defying blond hair, plump lips.

But he isn't paying me any attention. His gaze is fixed on Fran.

Fran takes a deep breath but before he gets a chance to give Shawn the spiel about how he needs to sign my pyjamas, Shawn closes the few feet between and hugs Fran. Fran stiffens, he doesn't move, doesn't return the hug.

'What are you doing here?' says Shawn, freeing him. Fran doesn't get a chance to tell him. Someone from Shawn's entourage interrupts us, calling the pop star. A serious-looking woman with an earpiece says, 'It's getting rough out there, Shawn! We need to leave immediately or we'll have to get a heli again.'

'Not the heli.' Shawn frowns petulantly. 'You know Jonathan hates flying.'

The woman looks at us. 'Then we have to leave *now*.'

'Okay.' Shawn turns to us. 'The longer we stay here the more of an avalanche forms outside. We have to get out now. You want to tell me what the hell you're doing here over dinner?'

Fran somehow finds his voice. 'Yeah, of course, let's go.'

The noise as we leave the stadium through the back exit is deafening. There are fans lined up and screaming. Rows of crying faces stream by me as I hold Fran's hand and feel the guiding touch of a bodyguard behind me. Photographers snap pictures by the dozen, creating a lightning storm in our face. I stumble a little. It's extremely disorienting and I suddenly have a glimpse of how overwhelming this life could be. Shawn lingers, trying his hardest to sign as many magazine covers, notebooks, banners and other things that he can. I can see he's anxious, too. He looks up at a fan, and a simple acknowledgement of her existence from Shawn turns her into a shaking wreck of tears. People tug at him, pinch him, pull at his neck. It looks terrifying. But Shawn never frowns or shows any sign of discomfort. He's a complete pro.

Fran and I hang back awkwardly, trying to stay out of any paparazzi or fangirl photos. I wonder if people are wondering who we are, or if they've even noticed us outside Shawn's glow.

It's not long before the pressure from the fans threatens to overturn the metal barriers, and I see a guard pushing Shawn towards the car as the others form a human shield around us. I look at Fran. He seems surprised by this; it's almost like he didn't quite realize that the fame was such a tangible thing. It's beautiful, but brutal and petrifying.

Shawn enters the car first, followed by a handsome Asian man, about our age, with an earring and perfectly applied winged liner. He's clutching an expensive-looking make-up box. I follow afterwards with the woman with the earpiece close behind. The last to get in are Fran and the two bodyguards that seem to be part of Shawn's private security. Fran sidles up next to me in the back row and grabs my hand.

'You okay? That was intense,' he whispers in my ear. I nod, lost for words. It's all happening so fast. How did we go from wanting Shawn to sign my PJs to being squashed in a car beside him?

The screams follow us and people bang on the windows mercilessly; they even try the door handle, but it's locked. Shawn seems relaxed, as if this is second nature to him. Eventually, we leave the crowd behind and the last running, screaming fan falls back, unable to trail us any longer.

'Restaurants don't offer any privacy. Want to come back to mine and eat there?' Shawn says to Fran, as if this is the most normal thing ever.

Fran shrugs non-committally and I stay quiet, scared of breaking whatever magic is happening right now.

Shawn's house is even grander than the one Fran and I tried earlier. It's part glass, with a long white minimalist driveway that swirls into view after we pass the guarded gate. Shawn gets out of the car and waltzes up to the entryway. He opens the heavy door and his make-up artist, whom he introduced as Jonathan in the car, types a code into the security system. The house is humongous and slightly eerie for all the moonlight it lets in. The lady with the earpiece, whom Shawn introduces as Susan, follows us closely.

'My chef will be here any minute, what do you all want? Is sushi okay?' Shawn asks.

He looks at Fran and then at me. We both nod. I'm not sure what else you would say when someone offers you sushi made by their private chef.

'He's great, he's from Kyoto,' Shawn continues. 'Jonathan discovered him. He makes this killer fatty tuna roll. It's going to blow you away.'

Shawn talks fast. Almost as if he's trying to prove something, like he's nervous. But that's impossible, how could *we* make Shawn Next nervous? The practised seductive Shawn that I know so well from interviews, the one who would bite his lip sometimes while looking up at the camera through thick lashes, is gone. He seems more boyish now, eager and kind and fast-talking. 'Unless you don't like fatty tuna, he can make something else?'

He's looking directly at Fran.

'No, no, I love fatty tuna,' Fran says vacantly. I'm pretty sure he's never had fatty tuna before. He is still looking up at the high ceilings with disbelief, his face set hard as if he's stumbled into a dream. Or a nightmare.

'Okay cool, because he can make literally anything,' Shawn continues nervously. His friend Jonathan gives him a reassuring look.

The idea of Shawn Next trying to impress me makes me want to giggle.

When his chef arrives, Shawn orders enough sushi for twelve people then gives us a tour of his house. I've hardly said four words since his bodyguards stopped chasing us and I found myself in a literal fantasy. I've never wanted Lizzy to be with me more than in this moment. This was beyond any of the *what if* scenarios we used to giggle over while staring up at her Shawn Next posters.

There's a Skittles machine, artwork from a famous graffiti artist, a wine cellar that seems to have come with the house and that Shawn has little interest in. Though he does keep a special branded Dr Pepper fridge full of Dr Peppers there. I grin at Fran and point. Fran doesn't smile back.

There's a pool outside, and a sweeping view of Los Angeles. I'm quiet for most of the tour as Shawn and Fran make small talk. *How's the home town? Does the pigeon lady still guard the town hall? Whatever happened to next-door neighbour Janet?*

Eventually we settle into the giant L couches in his living room, facing each other over of a small sea of sushi.

CHAPTER 21

NDAs and tuna rolls

'This sushi is amazing,' I say dipping my umpteenth roll into the adorable little soy sauce dish that has been laid out next to me.

'Isn't it?' Jonathan exclaims gleefully. 'Chef Haruko is so talented.'

Jonathan is very elegant, and so refined, that I feel myself adjusting my posture in front of him. He's wearing a stylish purple silk blouse with tight jeans; his fingers are long and neat. With his eyeliner still intact, he looks every inch the glamorous celebrity that Shawn is.

'The tuna was fresher last time,' Susan grumbles. Jonathan shoots her an irritated look.

'Nothing is ever perfect enough for our dear Susan,' he laments. But he's smiling at her now.

'My job is to be critical and make sure everything is perfect enough for Shawn,' she fires back.

'Your job is to manage, not micromanage,' says Jonathan playfully.

I'm trying to crack the dynamics between the three of them and failing miserably.

Fran is eating in silence, and I'm wondering at which point he is going to warm up. Or open up. Or say anything. I hold his hand but he doesn't squeeze back, just leaves it lying limply in mine. He's been like this since Shawn hugged us at the concert and whisked us away, like he's found himself in a situation he can't make sense of.

Shawn seems to have come to the same conclusion. He eyes Fran and clears his throat.

'So, Franny, tell me what you have been up to. How are things at home?'

Fran stiffens a little at the question. 'Everything has been ... okay,' he lies. He shuffles some seaweed salad around his plate before continuing.

'Dad is on his second tour in the Middle East. I dropped out of high school to work but I'm almost done with community college. I get good grades so maybe I can transfer somewhere ...'

Shawn pretends to focus on his miso soup. 'And how is your mom?' he says with forced nonchalance. Jonathan and Shawn exchange a loaded look but Fran misses it entirely because he's fiddling with his chopsticks.

I'm frozen to the spot. What is going on here? How am I sitting in THE Shawn Next's house, eating spicy tuna with his entourage, hand in hand with a guy I'm crazy about, while the two of them talk in stilted tones like two old ladies making polite small talk in church?

'My mum is okay,' Fran replies. More lies. 'How about you?' he asks, eager to change the subject from his mother. 'How are fame and fortune treating you?'

I tense. I think he was trying to be light-hearted but it came out sounding like a shot.

'There are a lot of good sides and bad sides,' says Shawn. 'I don't have any privacy most of the time, and I'm always watched. No offence, Susan.'

'None taken,' his manager fires back. 'I don't watch, I protect. You'll thank me someday.'

'But,' Shawn continues, 'I'm able to give my parents a

really good life, and there are other obvious perks as well. Plus, you know I love singing.'

'How are Don and Carole?' Fran asks, still concentrating on his food and utensils in order to avoid eye contact. I recognize the names of Shawn's parents, from the bus tour, and the biography. Shame reddens my cheeks, even though there is no way for Shawn to know that I literally stalked his mom and dad.

'They are doing great. You know what, they would love to see you. We should go see them.' Shawn smiles at the thought.

Fran is silent for a moment. He rolls his eyes. 'Yeah, right. I'm sure they would love to see me.' His sarcasm is so palpable that a wave of awkwardness washes over everyone present.

Shawn glares at him. 'What's that supposed to mean?'

'I just ...' Fran pushes his chopsticks away and finally locks eyes with his former best friend. 'I don't understand what the point is of lying about that. Your parents would not love to see me, neither you nor your parents ever cared about me at all, so just ... why lie? Why say that?'

'My parents and I did care about you,' Shawn counters glacially.

'Are you serious?' Fran's temper is rising, I can feel it. 'You never spoke to me again, never reached out after you left. Not once. How can you say you cared?'

Shawn is quiet before saying, 'I tried contacting you many times, Fran.'

'Just stop lying,' Fran thunders, releasing my hand. I flinch at his tone.

This time Shawn loses his temper and he gets up abruptly too. Jonathan looks on, anxious despite his prim composure. 'I called you loads of times. And when I realized you didn't want to talk to me, my management told me to drop it. Didn't want you blackmailing me.'

Fran shoots up to his feet too. 'Liar!' he bellows. 'Where were these mysterious calls? When did I say I wanted nothing to do with you? And what the hell would I blackmail you over?'

Fran and Shawn stare daggers at each other, anger coursing between them like a real tangible thing. Susan, Jonathan and I have all stopped eating.

'Your mom picked up, every time,' says Shawn. 'She kept saying you were unavailable, and the very last time I called she said I was bad for you, and that you didn't want to be around people like me.'

I can see the pain on Shawn's face, and Jonathan seems to see it too; he gazes regretfully up at his friend.

Fran looks confused. 'People like you? What does that even mean?'

Shawn shoots a loaded look at Jonathan. Then he sighs and carries on.

'The kiss, Franny. Remember? The time I tried to kiss you? I thought that's why you didn't want to be friends with me any more.'

A piece of sashimi falls silently from my chopsticks to my plate. Wait. What?

Fran stares at Shawn then at Jonathan as if they are privy to some inside joke that he doesn't understand. Susan looks down at her plate and I stuff the tuna into my mouth, hoping my chewing will stop me interrupting the drama with gasps of disbelief.

'Huh?' Fran says. 'What kiss?'

'Maybe we should all settle down, take a breather,' Susan offers.

'Stay out of it,' Jonathan snaps.

'In eighth grade, in your backyard. I kissed you,' Shawn continues.

Awkwardly Fran nods. 'Yeah, so what? What does it matter?'

'Your mom saw us that day.'

Fran is still looking at everyone as if he doesn't understand anything.

'I always cared about you, Fran, I still care about you,' Shawn admits. 'I thought you wanted nothing to do with me because I'm gay.'

I'm kind of sad that Fran has never seen *The Notebook* because, aside from our Gosling kiss in the rain, this scene unfolding before us is giving me serious vibes. Shawn still cares about his old best friend! My insides give a little dance.

'Jonathan is my boyfriend,' Shawn says.

Jonathan gives Fran and me a little smile and wave as Susan's fingers tense around the fancy bamboo chopsticks, her entire career probably flashing before her eyes.

'I'm going to need them both to sign NDAs,' she declares, shark eyes intent on me. This is what she meant about protecting him.

'Not now, Susan,' Shawn snaps.

'My . . .' Fran's voice stumbles over itself, pain etched in every note. Tears are streaming down his face. I want to reach for him again, stand beside him and hug him, but I know he needs this moment, he needs to get everything off his chest. 'My mom is sick, she has paranoid episodes ... You know that. And I don't think she was referring to the kiss ... Well, maybe.' His voice hitches a little. 'I don't know. But after you left I really wanted to see you but she kept saying that it's dangerous to spend time with famous people, that it makes someone a target etcetera. She was really paranoid about your fame, but I had no idea you had ever spoken. I thought you just forgot me.'

Fran's breaths come in ragged spurts. Jonathan looks at me and the expression on his face tells me he wants to comfort his boyfriend too. This is hard to watch.

Both boys look so sad and deflated, an entire friendship lost over what could have been a misunderstanding. Or maybe Fran's mum's misguided attempt to shelter Fran from Shawn's rising fame. Or maybe something worse.

'My management put all these thoughts in my head,' Shawn says. 'I was so young, they were scared that news of my sexuality would leak if I wasn't careful. That it would end my career. They interrogated me about my past and they thought it best I not pursue our friendship if your mom was unhappy with it, since you knew about me. They were scared of the scandal it could bring.'

'Why would I not want you in my life just because

you're gay? *You*,' Fran points angrily at Susan. '*You* did this?'

Shawn puts his hand out. 'No, no, it wasn't Susan. I have new management now.' He smiles at her. 'Susan lets me live my truth, and she knows about my relationship with Jonathan,' he adds.

'But you're not public?' I blurt out.

'Not yet.' Shawn gives Jonathan a meaningful look. Jonathan flashes him a knowing smile. As if they have plans.

'But I'm not hiding any more,' says Shawn. 'I no longer have fake PR relationships. I was scared before, I was so young and my entire brand was tween girls . . . My parents didn't even know about me and I was still figuring it all out for myself. But I'm ready now, I'm finally strong enough.'

I swear I hear Susan mumble something about NDAs again.

'I got rid of the toxic people in my life,' Shawn continues. 'I'm much better now, surrounded by good people who care about me. But when I became famous I was so lonely, I made some big mistakes. I did things I shouldn't have, and my team kept me isolated. I couldn't be myself. I was a wreck. Maybe it's best I wasn't in your life, Fran.'

I remember Shawn's dark phase all over the press; they loved building him up then watching him fall. He was caught with drugs, driving on the wrong side of the road, throwing crazy parties. Paparazzi would take photos of him looking half passed out in the back of various cars, huge headlines screaming about how his career was over even though they were the ones making it worse. Lizzy would always say that everyone should be trying to help him, not enjoying watching him destroy himself, because he was clearly *going through something*.

Turns out she was right.

Fran wipes his tears away. 'After you moved my life fell apart, Shawn. Mom walked out on us, *again*. We couldn't find her so Dad just left and went to Syria so he didn't have to deal with things at home.' Fran starts shaking. 'There was no one left. And I . . . I guess I needed you. I needed a friend.'

'I asked my parents to give you my address,' Shawn says. 'When they had to move because that crazy fan broke into their house. I asked that they give you my address, so that that door was always open for you. If you needed me.'

'I thought that was like to forward your mail or something.' Fran scratches at his hair.

'You're stupid, you know that?' says Shawn, but his tone is back to being affectionate and warm. 'We had to move from the next house too though. It's hard to stay anywhere for too long, people are too good at sleuthing.'

'This house is way nicer by the way,' I say, looking around the room.

Everyone turns to me as one, surprised I can actually speak. Fran looks like he'd forgotten I was even there.

Susan's eyes narrow on me predatorily. 'How do you know that?'

'Susan, please stay out of this,' Shawn begs.

'Hold on, Shawn.' Susan puts her hand up. 'Something doesn't add up here. I want to know what they were actually doing at the concert, and why they've seen your old house.'

'I should have fought harder to be in touch with you, Fran, to keep contact,' says Shawn, ignoring his manager.

'He talks a lot about you,' adds Jonathan. Fran looks overwhelmed and a little sick but he smiles at this news.

I know it hurts him that this whole thing was his mother's doing. But it probably feels good not to think that Shawn forgot about him. Hesitantly, Fran takes a step towards Shawn and embraces him. Shawn Next hugs him right back.

'Now can I ask them why they were at your house?' Susan grumbles, ruining the moment.

Fran and I tell them everything about the trip. I start with Lizzy, which has Jonathan dabbing his eyes, then move on to Aunt Larissa and getting mugged and missing Shawn in NYC.

'Wait. So, it's because of *me* that you met Franny and ended up crossing half of America?' Shawn says, his mouth agape with disbelief.

Fran tells him not to flatter himself but Shawn looks at him as if to say *You owe me for being your matchmaker.* Fran kisses my cheek and makes me blush.

Jonathan and Shawn laugh hysterically when we tell them about the frappuccino incident, and the Uranus Candy Factory, and my mistaking Fran for a donkey.

'And that's why we were at Shawn's old house,' I conclude to Susan, who sniffs and nods curtly as if finally satisfied by the explanation.

Shawn is sitting back on his couch, his arm casually

draped around Jonathan, who has his hand on Shawn's knee. Shawn's shaking his head slowly at Fran.

'You sold the Cadillac?' he says eventually in disbelief. 'For concert tickets?'

Fran gives me a sheepish look. 'It was all worth it.'

'Oh my God. Seriously. That is the cutest story I've ever heard.' Jonathan clutches his heart. 'It's like a movie!'

Fran and I look at one another and he takes my hand, telling them about Venice and me throwing myself into the sea and how the darkest days of our lives have led us here, at the end of the longest journey, together.

Shawn moves to sit beside me and I fight my inner fangirl to stay calm.

'Well I guess it's time,' he says.

'Time for what?' I ask.

He smiles wide. 'Time to finally get those pyjamas signed.'

CHAPTER 22

To Lizzy

'Tell me what she was like,' Shawn asks as we stand in his luxurious kitchen. He fetches a Sharpie from a drawer.

I try to control my voice to keep from crying. 'She was pretty, and kind, and wild, and funny. Funny most of all. *Laugh till you pee your pants* kind of funny.'

'My favourite sort of person,' he says.

I smile up at him. My crush is gone, the real person is so much better.

Shawn takes the Sharpie and gently straightens the pyjama top over the marble of the island. I watch him slowly write the words, and it's like he's writing them across my heart.

To funny Lizzy, with love, Shawn

To brave Nadia, with love, Shawn

I'm crying and I don't bother wiping my tears away. Fran's hands wrap around me from behind and he kisses my cheek.

'Your music meant so much to Lizzy,' I tell Shawn.

'Thank you, I'm glad,' he says, blue eyes settling on me. 'I'm really sorry for your loss.'

He says it genuinely. Like someone who has felt loss too. People recognize loss in each other. There are those of us who have felt it, and those of us who haven't. I realize now Fran has felt it too. The shape and type of loss doesn't matter, it's not quantifiable. I feel guilty for not seeing that sooner. For not realizing that he needed to find something on this journey too.

Shawn squeezes my hand.

He knows what it's like to miss a best friend. I can see there were moments when Shawn looked into the crowd and wished Fran was there.

When Jonathan goes to bed and Susan leaves, I give the boys some privacy to properly catch up.

I wander in and out of the mansion's many rooms, showing them to Lizzy.

'And this is his bathroom,' I whisper. 'Remember how we used to joke about how it would be impossible for him to bathe because he was so perfect he probably walked on water?'

'And this is the best part,' I say to her, pointing to Shawn's proudly displayed Grammy, his MTV Awards, photographs from his concerts.

I look at the photos on his wall, the memorabilia and the framed press cuttings and golden records, marvelling at how all these things he's experienced were shared between Lizzy and me too.

That night Fran and I have a massive suite all to ourselves, a bedroom bigger than most apartments. It even has a couch and two TVs!

Fran has changed. It's like being with a lighter, new-and-improved version of the guy I've spent the last week with. He's full of energy and we dance and laugh and kiss. I tell him I'm sorry for being so mean before, and he tells me he's sorry for being so closed off ... Thanking me for giving him this opportunity to heal too. And although neither of us says it, it feels like fate that all the darkness we have experienced led us to one

268

another and to this moment where everything seems so much brighter.

We soak for ages in the giant jacuzzi bath, and Fran tells me more stories about his childhood with Shawn, and I tell him more stories about Lizzy, and the pain we've carried along the whole of Route 66 begins to float away with the steam.

'I think we should count this as skinny-dipping on your list,' Fran murmurs, kissing my soapy shoulder.

'I agree.'

I feel like a movie star. I wish I could bottle this feeling in a snow globe, shake it every time I want it again. I know we don't have a lot of time left together. That we are running out of it. But I don't let the fear suck me in; in this moment we are infinite.

I fall asleep in his arms on the unnecessarily large California king bed, sheets draped around me like a toga.

CHAPTER 23

Airplane and champagne

'I hope you're hungry,' Jonathan announces as Fran and I sheepishly emerge from our room. The beautiful kitchen island is littered with croissants, pitchers of orange juice, poached eggs and trays of delicately cut avocado.

'You cooked all of this?' I say wide-eyed.

Shawn snort-laughs. Jonathan sticks his tongue out at his boyfriend.

'I art directed all of this,' Jonathan explains, smiling. 'My food ordering skills are legendary.'

'Where is Susan?' Fran asks, settling by the island. Shawn bites into a croissant. 'I gave her some time off.

We are going on vacation today, to the South of Italy. I need a break from her anyway.'

'Oh.' Fran tries to fake a smile, but I can tell that *oh* is so jam-packed with disappointment. I think he wants more time with Shawn. More time to get to know the person his best friend has become.

'These are for you by the way,' Shawn adds, casually setting a white box in front of me and one in front of Fran. I stare down at it in disbelief.

'That's too generous.' Fran pushes the iPhone back towards Shawn.

Shawn pushes the box back stubbornly. 'Don't be a pain, Franny.'

'Thank you so much!' I say, awestruck. I've never owned a phone that wasn't a hand-me-down and now I own the latest freaking iPhone!

'And I've been thinking,' Shawn continues, 'how about you both join us in Portofino?'

Portofino in Italy? Like the hang-out of Kardashians and supermodels and Hollywood stars?

What's next? A yacht? A midnight shutdown of Tiffany's? I feel like Shawn is re-enacting that Oprah meme where she screams at everyone that they get a car.

'I would love to honestly,' I say, 'but I really, *really*,

have to go home. My family has probably already alerted all forms of authorities and I still need to figure out how I'm getting back.'

It's been one full day since I've let them know I'm safe. Probably a lifetime in the eyes of a parent. My stomach flips and I feel nauseous. As soon as we finish breakfast I need to get to an airport.

'I understand. How about you?' Shawn looks at Fran, hopeful.

'I . . .' Fran stutters and looks at me. As if he needs my approval for this. I turn to Shawn and grin.

'Fran is completely free!'

Shawn taps the counter in celebration. 'Okay, it's settled!' He looks at me mischievously. 'If you won't come with us then at the very least allow me to give you a lift home?'

I've obviously never been on a private jet before. I've never even seen one up close, or up far, but now that I have, I think I will really have a hard time flying with anyone else.

Everything is so clean, and the interior sparkles in tones of beige and luxurious brown. The stewardess is beautiful and the airline has brought us In-N-Out for lunch, which I guess is one of those celebrity requests Shawn can make. The meat-and-cheese-topped animal fries and double double cheeseburgers are to die for and are served on real china plates! Before take-off I turn my phone on and write my final text message to Larissa and my parents.

> I'm on a plane. I'm coming home.

When we hit cruising altitude Jonathan asks to see Lizzy's physical list. I show it to him and he folds it flat, reading it with deep concentration.

'Yes! I was hoping there would be something on here that I could help you cross off,' he says, contemplating the list, 'just to be part of this whole epic experience of yours . . . and there totally is something!'

Giddily, Jonathan points at number 15 – *toast with expensive champagne*. 'We have Cristal on board!' he announces with a squeal.

Fran looks at me, eyes wide, and I giggle. Champagne and burgers on a private jet? One part of me can't wait to tell everyone I've met about this, while the other part wants to keep it a secret between Fran and me for ever.

The stewardess brings us flutes of bubbly and we toast.

'To Lizzy!' Jonathan exclaims.

'To Lizzy!' we all echo back.

I take a long swig, the bubbles tickling my nose. I dab at my eyes. Noting that happy tears feel so much better than the sad ones.

On the flight Fran helps me set up my new phone and we play Uno and drink more champagne till our vision goes blurry. When everyone on board has fallen asleep, I go on one of my little brain walks.

All I felt at Lizzy's funeral was anger.

I felt on display and like I was forced to be part of a performance. Angry that none of it felt comforting, even though I knew it was designed to be.

I felt nothing as I stood there staring at the coffin.

It's a weird thing to want to be acknowledged at your best friend's funeral.

It wasn't that I wanted attention. I wanted nothing more than to crawl under the covers in my room and hide. But I also wanted to feel entitled to the pain that I felt. To be told that I was entitled to the pain more than others.

But my mum called me to dinner that night like she

would have any other day, and complained about the untidy bathroom, and pushed me to go back to school.

I remember that anger. Hot and searing, pulsating through me. Rocking me like a wicked lullaby.

Everyone has that first moment when they realize the person they loved is actually gone. For me it was when I saw her name on a gravestone.

Her name shouldn't be on that stone. The words made it real for me. The closed coffin made it real for Lizzy's mum, who collapsed in a small sea of people when she heard the lid slam shut.

I push these memories away. I'm surprised to feel that the anger isn't as sharp any more. That for once I don't want to cry. The grief isn't gone, but it's a little muted. I can examine these memories and think about what they meant. I feel this lightness inside of me now, something that feels a lot like hope.

I look out of the window and I see London.

Fran takes hold of my hand as we land.

CHAPTER 24

Before you

Outside the plane I ask Fran to take a photo of Shawn and me.

'Is this for the list?' Fran asks, snapping the pic. I grin and nod and he seems pleased that this time he's not the one pushing me to cross something off.

I look different in the photo. Kind of older, which sounds weird because I've only been away a little over a week, but I feel like who I was at the start of this trip was years younger.

I ask Shawn if it's okay to post it and he happily agrees. For once I want to be the one to initiate crossing something off the list. I try not to grin too broadly and give the camera my best model face.

'I'll give you lovebirds some privacy,' says Shawn when we are done. He gives me a parting hug, then shoots Fran a naughty grin. Yes, he's a superstar, but he's also a boy, grinning stupidly at his best friend. I smile.

'See you soon, N.' He does a salute and goes up the stairs and back into the jet.

'See you soon, S!' I call after him.

I try to not squeal at the fact that Shawn Next and I have nicknames for each other. Jonathan pops his head out of the hatch and blows me a kiss then disappears.

It's easy enough to refocus on Fran. His hands are in the pockets of his jeans.

'So, Shawn said he could get me an interview at NYU. He has contacts in the film department.'

'That's amazing,' I say. And I mean it. I feel happy for him, happiness spreading through me like something hot and gooey.

'I would be closer to my abuela as well. Just one hour away.'

'Better get your house shoes ready.' I grin up at him. His hands wind around my hips, pulling me closer to him. I don't want to cry again, because I've done enough of that lately. But also, I'm going to miss him. Not just how he looks and the touch of his hands on my face and waist, but his smell and the sound of my name on his lips.

'He, *ummm*, also said I could stay in his empty apartment in New York. I said it was all too much but he insisted. Do you . . .' Fran hesitates. 'Think that's okay?'

'Absolutely.' I beam. He deserves this. He deserves it all. Fran smiles lightly. I can see that he's excited. Hope swirls around him like a glittering mist. He does that rocking back and forth thing again.

'New York is a six-hour flight to London,' he offers finally. My heart threatens to beat right through my chest.

'I know. That's how this all started, remember?'

He scratches his brown hair, giving me a lopsided smile. 'Would you . . . like to maybe come spend Thanksgiving with me?'

My stomach plummets and my jaw drops. 'Really? In New York?'

'Yeah, if they accept me, I'll go and get set up and you can come visit me during break.'

'My family would kill me if I go visit a boy in America.'

'Surely, they won't kill you for visiting your *boyfriend* in New York. We will drink a couple mocha frappa somethin' somethin's'. It will all be very innocent.'

It's the best phrase I've ever heard. I put my arms around his neck and kiss him.

'You sure you want a girlfriend?' I nod at the plane. 'With your *best friend of pop star, Shawn Next* title restored, you'll have your pick of groupies. You're easy on the eyes, you know.'

I'm half joking but it is something I've thought about. I think about girls like Ashley and Savannah.

His face gets serious all of a sudden and he looks down at me.

'Nadia, before you, I forgot what it was like to want to be with someone. I was so used to being alone. I know you came to the US trying to save yourself, but you ended up saving me. You ended up giving me hope.'

I'm not inwardly squealing any more. My heart feels full and like it's breaking at the same time. Tears stream down my face and Fran wipes them with his thumbs.

'And before I met you I'd forgotten what it was like to feel happy,' I tell him. 'I thought I would never feel happy again.'

He kisses me, deeply, again and again, holding my face cupped in his hands. Until we realize we are clearly making a show of ourselves. Mentally I had crossed off the kiss after the desert, but no. *This* is it. This is my true Gosling kiss.

'I'll see you soon,' he says.

'You will.'

I walk away and get into the car that's waiting for me. We drive off.

I take one look back at the beautiful boy waving from the private jet's stairs.

CHAPTER 25

The stillness of my grief

I stand outside my home. I check the photo of Shawn and me that I posted on Instagram. There are 7453 likes already. Does that count as going viral? I think Lizzy would say so. Another thing off the list.

I smile even though my stomach is an icy pool of dread. I look up at our house. In this area no one has their own walls, we all share them via rows of identical terraced backyards, distinguishable only by the contents of the washing lines or the plastic toys that have been left out.

I take out my key with a shaking hand and fit it in the

lock. Before I'm done turning the key the door whips open and Mama stands there.

'Nadia.' She says my name with relief but she doesn't reach for me.

She stares for a few moments before speaking. 'Your hair is blue.'

She's still for a few more seconds, then her arms close around me like iron. The air blows out of me as she squeezes my ribs so hard that I feel like they might crack. She sobs once into my shoulder, loud and hard, holding on to me for dear life.

Just as I think that maybe she is less angry with me than I thought, she pushes me away.

'How could you?'

I stare briefly at the cement porch. Then I lift my chin. She repeats her question even though I know it's rhetorical.

I don't know how I could. I just did. I *needed* to.

'I'm sorry, Mama.' That's all I offer.

Things go quickly after that. I'm ushered into the house. Hands flutter around me. Taking off my coat, throwing my bag and suitcase aside. I catch a glimpse of my brothers. They wave but they stay away. They know I'm in a world of trouble and they don't want to get caught in the fallout. They'll say hi when I'm done being yelled at. It's a younger sibling defense mechanism. I'm pushed into the sitting room.

My father looms over me.

'We thought you were dead, Nadejda,' he thunders. He's a man of very few words and he almost never uses my full name. His tone is ice, his eyes are glazed . . . with tears? A vein throbs in his neck. I've never seen this much rage in him and he looks exhausted.

'Do you know what it's like to think your daughter is dead?' His voice is even louder now.

I tried to let you know I was safe, I want to say. But I know a text or voice note isn't enough when your teenage daughter disappears.

'I was as good as dead when I went,' I say quietly.

My mother's lips are pinched. 'What does that mean?' She turns to my dad. Her voice goes hysterical. 'What does that mean, Vassily?'

Her voice grows even more hysterical when she turns back to me. 'I cannot believe Larissa let you go!' she says. 'I could kill her. I nearly did when she said you weren't coming back yet. And those messages you left us! Were they meant to be reassuring?'

I sink further into the worn-down couch. I feel bad for putting Larissa in this much trouble.

'I thought you were dead, sold to someone!' Mama continues.

'Well which one is it?' I snap. 'You can hardly be both.'

I regret my cheek instantly. I believe that she was scared, I believe that she was worried. But I don't have any room for her anger. I feel like all I've gotten from her in these last few months is her disappointment. I need her to see *me*. To take herself out of the equation for a minute and to see that I've cried every day for months on end.

'How dare you be rude to your mother after what you put her through? After how you made her feel?' Papa demands.

'I love you, that's why I worry!' says Mama angrily.

'I know you love me, Mama.' This time I sob as the pain rocks through me, sudden and unexpected. 'I know. But I needed you to love me *more* through this. I needed to talk about it. I needed you to hold me. I need you to acknowledge what happened. Not to tell me to be strong over and over again.'

'Strength is all we have,' my dad says. Another sob breaks free from my insides, as if ripped from there.

'Why would I not want you to be strong?' Mama asks, as if repeating a complicated riddle. She notices Stepa's sweater on the couch and starts to fold it.

'Mama, stop.'

I don't know if it's Soviet wiring or what, but there is always something she needs to be doing, something to be done. There is no room for pity, or slowing down, or sitting down to cry. She doesn't physically have room for the stillness of my grief.

'Where I grew up,' she tells me, 'if you felt sorry for yourself, even for a minute, you were dead.'

'I'm not a soldier!' My voice rises. The sobs grow louder. Shuddering through me like tiny eruptions. The thickness in my throat chokes me. 'I'm your grieving daughter!' I shout. I look at my papa and speak more quietly. 'A part of me died this year, Papa, with Lizzy!'

The words hit exactly where they needed to.

I watch as his face crumbles from one of stern anger to pain and fear, of the realization that his little girl couldn't simply tough this one out. His icy blue eyes are glistening; a tear rolls down one cheek.

His fist is clenched, not in anger at me but in anger at the world for hurting me in this way. I am surprised when I hear Mama cry too. Her sobs are quiet. She looks at me as if she hasn't seen me before. Her lashes are wet.

'I'm sorry, *sontze*,' she says; it means *sunshine*, my childhood nickname. 'I'm sorry you have this pain.

I wish I could take it away, I ... When Tomya died in a car crash ...'

I look over at her, surprised by her mention of the dead brother she never talks about.

'When Tomya died, my world was ripped apart. He was my best friend. The only way to get over it was to get through it, so we just kept going, we didn't stop to feel any of it, and I thought ...' Her sobs grow stronger now. 'I thought that maybe if I kept you busy with everyday stuff, if we just kept you going forward you would get through this faster.'

My heart softens a little. 'Mama, sometimes we can't keep going. Sometimes we need to stop and feel.'

She hugs me. Which feels a little alien to me, but I relax into it because this is what I craved for so long. I cry into her arms.

I feel Dad get up and he puts a hand on my shoulder. He kisses the top of my head. Just like that the magic has passed. But something in me feels better. Lighter.

Though I can tell I'm back to being in massive heaps of trouble.

After my brothers come and give me a hug my mum informs me that I am grounded for real this time. She also tells me that I will have to cook dinner twice a week for a month, I will not get an allowance and I will have to help Dad with his work on Fridays.

I don't mind too much because frankly I was afraid they would take my new phone away, or my computer, and that I would have no way to talk to Fran. I almost kind of feel like I pulled a fast one on them. I feel my phone vibrate gently in my pocket as the Instagram notifications keep rolling in.

When I'm back in my room the first thing I do is take a photo of Lizzy out from the box from under my bed. I put it in my school bag. I want to carry a photo of her with me from now on. I want to remember Lizzy and smile. I want to remember the lines of her face.

When I've calmed down and unpacked I sit in my room, the Shawn Next PJs splayed next to me. I touch the cotton.

Stepa peeks his head into the room, brown hair dishevelled.

He waves his phone at me.

'Are we going to talk about this Instagram thing?' He grins. 'Thirty thousand likes and counting.'

Nikita's head peeks into the room from below Stepa. They are like stackable heads in my entryway.

'Did you REALLY ride in a private jet?' Nikita beams. I included that tidbit in my Instagram caption.

I smile conspiratorially and pat the bed. They both shuffle in.

I tell them everything. *Well*, everything aside from the night on Venice Beach. And the nights with Fran.

'I can't believe you've been to LA!' says Stepa with a sheer look of admiration.

'And seen Route 66!' yelps little ginger Nikita.

'How do you know about Route 66?' I ask incredulously.

'It's what that cartoon *Cars* is based on,' he informs me.

I make a mental note to tell Fran this fun fact.

I love seeing my brothers on my bed. Wide-eyed and eager, hungry for more stories.

I think about how long it has been since I gave them this love, this time. I've been too broken to give them anything.

'Let's have a sleepover in my room and I'll tell you everything about my trip, we'll watch a movie too,' I offer. 'We can watch that new Disney *Star Wars* show you both like.'

The boys go and grab blankets, and we all burrow in my bed. Against my mum's complaints I order burgers. She moans that we have a full kitchen but I ignore her.

I give my brothers the crystals I got for them on Route 66, and the funny candies I kept for them from the candy factory. Nikita finds the Uranus jokes especially hilarious.

At some point Mama joins us, and though the bed can barely fit him, Dad squeezes in too.

We cuddle and watch movies and eat our burgers.

I've missed them all so much.

CHAPTER 26

Hope, faith and pelmeni

It's my first Friday family dinner since I got back.

My uncle tells me I'm a disappointment. Larissa isn't coming, or isn't invited, I'm not sure which. I've texted her about one million apologies for what I've done but she said we have some talking to do. Mama is still mad at her.

I walk into the kitchen and find my babushka there. She has a golden icon set up on the windowsill, with some skinny Orthodox Church candles burning away next to it. I know the icon is for her son, Tomya. Tomya died before I was born and so I never spent much time thinking about him, until now.

She's folding dough in on itself, making pelmeni again. She irons out a piece of the dough, then dips her fingers in a silver bowl. Inside the bowl is a mixture of ground meat, onions, egg, grated carrots, and breadcrumbs. My gaze narrows on her missing fingers as she gets a dollop of meat and plops it in the middle of the dough square. She folds it carefully and pinches the edges, then she sets a perfect dumpling on a nearby tray.

'Nadinka,' she says, and her voice is honey dripping on my soul. She looks at me with sadness.

'*Privet, Babushka.*' I sit opposite her. I pull a fistful of dough and start to iron it out.

'You scared us,' she says. 'We didn't know if we would get you back.'

She looks at the icon. As if remembering what it's like to not get someone you love back. I start to cry.

'I'm sorry, Babushka. I didn't want to worry you. I was just so sad all the time ...'

She wipes her hands on her floral apron. There is still some flour on them.

She looks at me. 'Nadia, there will come a day, when the loss you feel on the outside becomes a forever presence on the inside.' She taps her heart. I let the phrase sink in.

I sob quietly and stare up at her icon. 'Is Tomya a forever presence now?'

'Yes, I believe he is always with me,' she says. She starts making pelmeni again. She believes. Like her namesake – Viera, which means *faith*. That's all she has.

And all I have is hope – *Nadejda*. My namesake. Hope that I won't always feel this way. Hope that I will be happy. A hope that grows brighter and more real every day.

'Can you tell me about Tomya while we finish the pelmeni?' I ask.

Babushka smiles at me, revealing her two golden teeth. I can't believe I've never asked to hear about him before. I want to know about her forever presence, and I want to tell her about Lizzy too. My beautiful grandma who always let me sit on her lap, even when I became far too big to do so. I clasp her hand, despite mine being covered in flour.

Then she tells me everything. And we sit there, Faith and Hope, a sea of dough between us.

Making dumplings and sharing memories.

CHAPTER 27

Bingo she screams

I run from the bus stop through the rain. Larissa won't be happy that I'm late on top of everything else.

Sure enough, she stands under the hall's awning looking grumpy, her beautiful features twisted with displeasure. I haven't seen her since I came back, because I'm grounded and my mother isn't talking to her. So, I've asked her to meet me here, at the old community centre, and told my mum I had to volunteer.

'Why are we here?' She crosses her arms crabbily. 'It's pissing rain.'

'It's bingo night.' I point at the sign behind her.

'Remember? *Playing bingo with old ladies* is on the list.'

'This is a community centre,' Larissa counters, as if she'd much rather be on a posh high street.

'Yeah, well, I can't gamble yet so I won't be allowed in one of those bingo halls, this will have to do.'

It's only 5 p.m. but in the world of community centres and seniors this is prime night-time.

'Oh.' Larissa looks a little curious, but determined to still be angry with me. 'You owe me an apology!' she blurts out.

'I owe you a thousand apologies,' I say, taking her hand in mine. 'And a thousand thank yous too.'

Larissa seems to soften at this, blue eyes glinting.

'Look,' I continue. 'Playing bingo with old ladies is one of two last things on Lizzy's list and I thought maybe we could cross it off together?'

'Really?' Her anger seems to evaporate, in its place coming curiosity and excitement. She can't help herself. 'You got through most of the list?'

'I did, and I rode in a private jet, hugged a donkey, broke into a backstage area . . .'

'A private jet? Broke into where?' Larissa yelps.

'So, should we go in?' I point at the centre.

'*Fine*,' Larissa concedes grumpily, 'but I want to hear the ENTIRE story. No detail left out, not one single one.'

'Deal,' I smile.

Larissa looks very out of place inside the dusty old community centre. The former model struts in front of me. Her grey suede thigh-high boots slap against the linoleum as she throws back her cascading locks of brown hair. She buys us two orange squashes for a pound each at the makeshift bar and we take one of the free tables at the back.

I clock a few ancient men checking Larissa out. She winks at one and his dentures nearly fall on the table.

We settle and start marking the numbers called out. I tell her the entire story, leaving nothing out, not even the night in Venice. She's the only one I would tell this stuff to. Larissa listens intently, eyes bright and eager, interspersing my story with *No way* and *You did what?* She stops listening only to mark off numbers on her bingo card.

I give her the other crystal I picked up for her at the roadside honour-system shop.

'Fran sounds really nice,' she gushes. I show her a photo on my phone.

'Ooooh!' She fans herself with her bingo card. 'And handsome!'

'He is.'

'It sounds like you had an amazing trip, but my sister and brother aren't talking to me now, even Babushka isn't talking to me. I don't even know if I'm allowed to Friday-night dinners any more, not that it's such a great loss but still. You betrayed me, Nadia.'

'I'm sorry.' I feel tears pushing against my ducts. 'I'm so sorry, Larissa, the last thing I ever wanted to do is betray you. But I was losing myself, and you were right, I needed this.'

She eyes me speculatively. 'And you feel better now?'

'I do. I really do. I feel some sense of being able to look forward. Of looking ahead instead of looking back. I think that was Lizzy's plan with the list. To give me something to look forward to.'

I set the list on the table in front of me, and reach the pen out to her. Pointing at the bit we can cross off now.

'I was going insane,' I tell her.

She crosses off the *Play bingo with old ladies* bit on Lizzy's list, looking pleased despite everything.

'Sometimes we need to do something crazy to feel sane again,' she tells me. 'So what if I'm not allowed at

296

Friday-night dinner for a little while? Maybe this is the perfect time for me to go on that month-long Southeast Asia trip I've been eyeing.'

'Yellow blue bus,' I say to Larissa.

She smiles at me and says it back.

I grab her hand.

'Larissa, you saved my life.'

She looks at me with disbelief, her eyes watering. Then she looks down, as another number rings loudly through the hall. Larissa's eyes widen further.

'BINGO!' she screams.

CHAPTER 28

For Lizzy

A week later I receive a text from Fran.

Did you do it yet?

I'm back at school. The Shawn Next photo has caused my reputation to soar. People try to be friends with me. Even Marjorie smiles at me now. I don't smile back.

After school I walk. I'm not headed home though. My heart hurts as I walk the all too familiar path – past an off-licence, past the petrol station, past the post office . . .

I end up at the two-storey townhouse I've been

dreading. Just like ours, this one is squeezed between a row of identical townhouses. It's so familiar it hurts.

I've seen this place so many times, but I haven't seen it since Lizzy died.

Her house looks the same; the only difference is that the roses in the front garden look a little unkempt. A little left behind.

I make a mental note to offer Boris, Lizzy's dad, a hand in the garden.

I knock on the door. I ignore the familiar sound of my fist on the wood.

It's crazy how if you've heard a certain generic sound enough times – a person's footsteps, the creak of a bed, a cough, the sound of your fist on a specific door – it brings forth a memory. I let myself remember what came next – Lizzy opening this door, cheeks flushed, flustered from running down the flight of stairs, pink pyjamas on.

Natalia, Lizzy's mum, opens the door and her mouth drops a little.

I hold out the cheap carnations bouquet I got at the supermarket and instantly feel like a fool.

Why did I even get a bouquet of flowers? I just felt like a pack of chocolates didn't really say *I'm sorry I never visited you after your daughter died.* They don't have cards that say that either.

I didn't warn them I was coming, I thought that would be the guaranteed way to make me chicken out.

'I wanted to drop by and say hello,' I say in the most awkward way possible.

Natalia smiles. 'Nadichka,' she coos my name and her arms wrap around me. Behind her I can see the house, and a sob rocks through me instantly, loudly. I'm so ashamed. But I should have known this would happen. I should have known Lizzy's house would do this to me.

Natalia squeezes me harder as I sob louder into her shoulder. I'm pretty sure I'm leaking snot on her nice jumper. I'm so ashamed. I came here to try and comfort her, instead I'm the only one bawling. She leads me into the house and closes the door, still hugging me.

'*Vse horosho,*' she says – *everything is okay.* She ushers me deeper into the house and I wipe at my tears furiously. I'm so embarrassed but each thing in their hallway sets me off again, the coat hanger, the mirror, the shoe rack.

Boris enters the hallway and joins Natalia in calming me down.

God I'm a nightmare.

Finally, I do calm down, and after I apologize about

six billion times Boris leads me to the living room and Natalia goes to grab some food.

We sit in the living room, facing each other over the coffee table and a mountain of food – khachapuri, Napoleon cake, glass bowls of chocolates so familiar from my childhood.

Russian chocolate is not what I would call the best but somehow all the Russians I know go out of their way to the Russian store in a different town just to buy them. Brands like Little Red Riding Hood and Seagull. Their love for it probably dates back to the time when these were the only ones they could have in the Soviet Union.

I can't really judge. Lizzy and I were deeply attached to Jammie Dodgers and they are not works of art either. I open a Seagull and chew quietly.

Lizzy's parents both look genuinely happy to see me and I can't believe I thought they might hate me. I swallow and reach for the signed Shawn Next pyjamas, and pull them out of my bag.

I tell them everything. About Shawn. About the list.

I pull the list out and show it to them. And some photos

that I brought along. They hold each thing delicately, as if they were made of glass instead of paper.

'The list,' Natalia smiles. 'It's just so Lizzy.'

'I know,' I say.

'Lizzy would have been so excited that you met Shawn Next,' says Boris as he examines the signed pyjamas.

'I know,' I say again, this time with a smile.

We eat and talk a little more.

When it's time to say goodbye, I ask them a question. 'Why don't I visit you, once a week for dinner after netball? Maybe ... maybe that would be okay? It could be our thing?' I say awkwardly. Maybe they don't even want to see me for dinner and I'm just inviting myself.

'I could cook so it's less work for you?' I add.

Natalia's lip wobbles, and instinctively Boris puts a hand on her knee. To steady her. I wonder how many times he has done this in the past eight months. How many times his palm has cupped her knee.

'We'd like that,' she says finally. 'We'd like that very much. But leave the cooking to the pros,' she jokes.

Natalia gives me more food to take home than I can

reasonably carry but I know it's just her way of saying *I love you*, so I don't mind.

That was it. The last thing on Lizzy's list, the one I was most afraid to do. *Visit my parents.*

I text Fran.

> I did it. It went well.

> I knew you would :) My brave brave Nadia. I have a surprise for you.

His response was quick and I bite my lip. I'm not used to having a boy in my life texting me sweet things. I could definitely get used to it, though.

I go and feed the swans in Windsor. It hurts a little less this time. For each dried piece of bread, I recall a memory of Lizzy. I summon it to the surface.

The memories still hurt. A dull ache in the pit of my belly. But they also feel good. Really good.

Lizzy snort-laughing at Nando's.

Lizzy holding back my hair when I was vomiting in the bushes outside Teddy's sweet sixteenth as she serenaded me with *Frozen*'s 'Let it Go'.

The ring of her northern accent when she told catcallers

where to go with the weirdest insults.

The random words she used and bent to her will. She called my brothers *pumpernickel* and *sourdough* instead of Nikita and Stepa.

I smile.

Memories of her don't make me hollow now. They fill me up.

I watch the swans peck at the bread, their elegant white necks glittering.

I make a decision then. I won't let grief take my body. I won't let it take my heart.

I'll keep going.

For Lizzy.

I will scream *I remember* into the canyons instead of wanting to forget.

I smile as I walk home, beaming up at the sky, the world suddenly appearing so much brighter and full of colour.

As I round the corner, moments from my house, I spot a familiar head of dark hair.

I get closer and before I know what I'm doing I've broken into a run and it feels like I'm flying, my feet hardly touching the ground. He's running too and we collide, Fran's arms swinging around me, catching me mid-flight and spinning me round and round.

We slow down and he kisses me, long and tender, taking the last bit of my breath away.

I pull away, panting. 'What the hell are you doing here?'

'I convinced Shawn to stop in England on the way back from Italy. They're off shopping at some place called Harrods.'

I roll my eyes. It is so very Fran to have never heard of Harrods.

'I have twelve hours before we leave,' he adds.

I grin up at him. There's a lot we can do in twelve hours, even though I wish it were twelve days or weeks.

I kiss him again, and again. As if I could never get enough.

'So, you and Shawn are all good now?'

'Yeah, we had so much more time to talk through everything. I also spoke on the phone to Shawn's parents and they helped me figure out some stuff about my mom's condition and timeline. I think I've been ashamed to deal with it all. I didn't know how to ask anyone.'

I nuzzle into his jacket, and he holds me tighter.

'I'm so happy you got him back. You deserve to have

someone looking out for you. Everyone does.'

'Yeah, well, it's thanks to you.'

My voice is muffled in his jacket. 'Is not.'

He looks down at me, big brown eyes that linger cheekily on my lips before filling with a deep earnestness.

'I was a ghost town before I met you, Nadia.' Fran's smile is impossibly wide. Hopeful. He runs his thumb across my chin.

'Same. But not any more,' I manage, distracted by the feel of his broad chest. 'We are fully inhabited towns now. Gold rush towns.'

I can keep going now. Not just for this beautiful boy. Not just for Lizzy. But for myself too.

I am not shattered into a thousand pieces like I thought. I am still a little broken, but my cracks are filled with memories.

'I brought you something.' Fran reaches into his pocket and pulls out a key chain with onions on it. 'Got it in a small city in south Italy that seemed about as obsessed with onions as you are.'

I smile. Remembering the way Lizzy used to crinkle her nose when I ate my onions on rye.

I dangle the key chain. A beautiful memory tucked inside another of my boyfriend giving me a souvenir.

I pop it on my keys, then reach up and kiss Fran. The sun beats down on our faces as he takes my face in his palms.

I make a promise to myself then. A promise that I'll carry memories in my heart, not ghosts. I'll coat those memories in new ones. Just like this.

ACKNOWLEDGEMENTS

This book took years to write, but the first draft came after I lost my dad to cancer. And the second draft came after I lost both grandparents. This is inevitably a book about loss but it's also about hope and the journeys we go on to rebuild ourselves. I dedicate this book to anyone who has had to deal with the big C. It's not easy, to lose someone in that way. And to anyone who has grieved, be it a life lost or the loss of a friendship (like Fran.) I wanted you to know that after grief comes hope. I hope this book can lift some people up from the trenches.

I'd like to thank my agent Kesia Lupo at Donald Maass Literary, for believing in me and taking a chance on me and for being my WhatsApp Cheerleader. I will always be grateful you made my childhood dream a reality. I want to thank my editor Lucy Pearse for acquiring the book and helping bring out Fran's character and making the love story all that it could be. Lots of the swoon is thanks to you. To my team at S&S, it's a pinch me moment for me to know I'm with such an iconic publisher and amazing team, thank you for all that you do. Thank you to David at S&S for the dreamy cover.

To my mother, who was my writing champion from day one. My biggest believer. The absolute *you can be anything you want to be* kind of mom.

To my brothers Misha and Nicky, you are my dose of whimsy and easy love. Being a big sister is my favorite thing (maybe you will see yourself in these pages.)

Thank you to my co-author and ride or die Natali Simmonds, in you I found that sense of intense teenage friendship where I want to call you all the time to just to talk about nothing. You have been a lifeline. You are so special to me.

This is a novel about friendship. I believe *best friends* isn't something that ever fades, every "best" friendship I've experienced is conserved in my brain, beautiful memories that have formed the person that I am. Jewels that I hold up to the light. Thank you, Bella, for the sleepovers and pizza. Thank you, Anna and Marina, for making sure my teen years were the wildest on record. To Tatiana for the make-up sessions and Japanese tutoring.

To Stace for the years of laughter and Primark hauls. To my friends Bryony, Stoph, Karina and Kris who are always willing to listen to voice notes.

To supportive authors and wonderful humans Marve Michael Anson and Anna Waterworth. To Abiola Bello who said something kind when I needed to hear it most. To the people who always have something kind to say Rachel G, Kirsty, Pixie, and the whole Verity Knights and everyone who supported Wunderkids. To #teamlupo and sisterswives and the whole Camp YA crew, to Demet and her very grounding presence. To Wren James, who has seen many iterations of this book and helped shape it. And a big thank you to Simon James Green and Molly Morris, my early blurbs are so special to me. To supportive authors like Amy McCaw, Katie Webber, and Laura Wood. To Nina for the insights. To the whole of UKYA for the community support.

To my family. To Nino, and the Silvesters and to Suks and Sarah. To my honorary top model aunties who served as the inspiration for the aunt here, Yuliya, Larissa and Rosie. To my nieces and nephews who are my lens into youth but especially my honorary nieces Olivia and Isabelle for being my birds'eye into what's cool. Honorary mention to Justin Bieber's song *Lonely* because it made me see what kind of grief pop stars might feel. Thank you to all the librarians, bloggers, and readers, there's nothing without you.

To my grandparents, it took me 30 odd years to realize we are a very special brand of weird and I love it. To Victor, Irina, Lena for the stories, and the thrifting, and the love. To Valera who taught me an author was a real thing to be. To my great grandma Lela, the librarian. To Rudi, gone too soon. And to my Verachka, I still remember your smell, and what it was like when you made me pelmeni or lifted up the blanket to let me cuddle by your side. To my father, I carry every piece of you in my heart. *Yellow Blue Bus*, Papa. To our home unit David, Ezzy and Laika. David you have held my hand through so much grief, thank you. Our love story is my favorite. Ezzy you are the hope that came after the storm. Your name means *helper a*nd every day you help me see the world in a beautiful light.

Lastly thank you to you, reader, of all the books in the world you chose to read this one, and that means so much.

ABOUT THE AUTHOR

Jacqueline Silvester has lived all over the world, living in Sweden, France, Germany, LA, London and New York. As a result, she speaks four languages. She studied at the University of Massachusetts and the Royal Holloway, London. After graduating she wrote her first novel and began writing cartoon screenplays. She is the author of self-published novel Wunderkids trilogy and the co-author of The Blood Web Chronicles under the pen name Caedis Knight. *The Last Wish List* is her first romance. She lives in London with her husband, her excessive YA collection and a hyper husky named Laika.